THE SUMMONER'S HANDBOOK

TARAN MATHARU

With illustrations by
Nicholas Delort and *David North*

FEIWEL AND FRIENDS
NEW YORK

A FEIWEL AND FRIENDS BOOK

An imprint of Macmillan Publishing Group, LLC

175 Fifth Avenue, New York, NY 10010

Our books may be purchased in bulk for promotional, educational, or business use.
Please contact your local bookseller or the Macmillan Corporate and Premium Sales Department at
(800) 221-7945 ext. 5442 or by e-mail at MacmillanSpecialMarkets@macmillan.com.

Library of Congress Cataloging-in-Publication Data

Names: Matharu, Taran, author.

Title: The summoner's handbook / Taran Matharu.

Description: First Edition. | New York : Feiwel and Friends, 2018. | Series:
The summoner trilogy | Summary: A collection of writings partially or primarily
authored or compiled by common summoner James Baker, including his journal of his
time at Vocans and at the front, his Treatise on the Basics of Summoning,
The Demonology Codex, The Essential List of Spells, and A History of Hominum.

Identifiers: LCCN 2018002540| ISBN 9781250189554 (hardcover) |
ISBN 9781250189561 (ebook)

Subjects: | CYAC: Magic--Fiction. | Demonology--Fiction. | Fantasy.

Classification: LCC PZ7.1.M37645 Su 2018 | DDC [Fic]--dc23

LC record available at https://lccn.loc.gov/2018002540

Book design by Sammy Yuen

Feiwel and Friends logo designed by Filomena Tuosto

First edition, 2018

1 3 5 7 9 10 8 6 4 2

To my grandmothers,
Ketty and Balbir

contents

Foreword
written by Dame Fairhaven

When Lord Scipio asked me to transcribe this journal, I agreed that the text contained within these pages was of immense value to prospective summoners across our great land. However, as I began to copy down James Baker's words, I realized that I could also supplement his findings with the new information we have gathered over the past few years, thanks in no small part to Fletcher Raleigh, Sylva Arkenia, Cress Freyja and Othello Thorsager.

It is my hope that this book will help summoners, both young and old, to learn more about our craft. And perhaps, should their consciences permit, understand more of the rigors and tribulations that commoner students face when coming to Vocans.

THE JOURNAL OF
JAMES BAKER

Day 1

I am a summoner. My fingers tremble as I write these words, though whether it is the cobbled streets shaking my carriage or the excitement of that knowledge, I cannot be sure. I've said it aloud over and over, but it still doesn't feel real. So, I write this entry in my new journal, to see if I can convince myself.

It was a day like any other when the Inquisitors came. My father had just finished baking. I remember the bell ringing as our store door opened and thinking how strange it was that the customers had not seen the CLOSED sign hung on its front.

And the fear in my mother's voice as she called me down the stairs. I remember that. They wore black cassocks, as all Inquisitors do. I had seen them walking the streets, their demons often by their sides. Strange creatures to be sure, but today there were none present. I was thankful for that.

The first man introduced himself as Inquisitor Rook, the other, Inquisitor Faversham. They spoke in bored voices, as if their job here was a chore. I supposed it was—but who else could do it? Only a summoner could test for another summoner.

Still, they had come to see me. That was unusual. Normally the boys and girls who had come of age would be lined up to be tested, their names checked against a list by a guard outside. But I had been sick when it was my turn, and no Inquisitor would want to touch a contagious child. So they had come to my little town.

"Come here, boy," Rook had said, snapping his fingers. It seemed they were annoyed to have had to make a personal visit.

I stepped forward and took the hand he was holding out. And that was it. One moment, I was set to follow the vocation that was my namesake, like my father before me. The next, my blood was boiling in my veins, and the surface of my hand glowed blue as the winter sky. Then, I was a summoner. My life was changed forever.

They gave me but an hour to say good-bye to my family, and only then because my father offered them warm pastries for their return, saying it would be one more hour for them to finish baking.

My mother cried the whole time, and I must admit, at first I did as well. But when Faversham muttered the words, "sniveling wretch," I soon stopped.

She gave me this journal. It was a gift for next year, my sixteenth birthday. She said I would make better use of it now. I sit on the floor of the carriage, while the two Inquisitors sprawl asleep on the bunks on either side of me. My only comfort are the pastries, half-eaten and discarded by the Inquisitors. They are cold, but they taste like home. I shall miss it.

Day 2

Vocans. I did not know that was our destination until I heard the carriage driver shout its name, a muffled cry filtering through the velvet curtains of the carriage windows. It woke the Inquisitors, who cursed at him. But they did not stop me from pressing my face against the glass, to see the ancient castle in all its glory.

The building was made up of four rounded turrets above a square building, surrounded by a moat of dark water. I caught no more than a glimpse before we were trundling across its drawbridge. Moments later, the Inquisitors dragged me up the stairs within a dim, walled courtyard at the castle's front and into the hallowed halls of the castle proper.

Inside was a great atrium, held up by oak beams and lit by crackling torches in the walls as well as a round skylight in its ceiling. Five stories of balconies lay on either side of me, with winding staircases between them, and doors and corridors in the walls of each floor.

Opposite me, another set of double doors lay open, with benches and tables within. I could see students sitting and eating, but that was not what drew my eye. Above the doors were beautiful carvings of demons, their eyes set with jewels. The display was breathtaking, though I had barely a few seconds to look at it. Soon an impatient servant was leading me up the stairs.

I could hardly keep up, for the servant was in a hurry, ignoring my breathless questions. Even so, I could not help but stop and marvel at the great tapestries and paintings hung along the walls, as well as the armor that ancient warriors once wore.

One painting even depicted the famous Battle of Watford Bridge, and I found it very hard not to pause at the sight of an orcs' rhino charge being blasted aside by a heroic summoner in the midst of battle.

More fascinating still were the orcish weapons on display, great clubs studded with stones, as well as bone armor and feathered jewelry. Perhaps most interesting of all were the myriad demons floating in jars, the containers stacked in rows within glass cabinets.

The servant tutted and fretted the whole way, cursing me for taking so long. Soon, I was led to a small room in the west tower, at its very top.

There were plenty of rooms to choose from.

"Not many of you commoners this year," the servant said. "You're to stay here until after breakfast. The others will be up soon."

Then he left me.

Day 3

I met the other commoners today. In truth, I had hoped that we would become fast friends, but there seemed to be a petty rivalry that kept us apart, though rivalry over what, I could not tell. The others had been together for a week already, two boys named Valentine and Tobias, common fellows such as myself, and a girl called Juno. Yet the trio seemed more acquaintances than companions, even after all that time together, and the three seemed sullen at my presence.

It gave me little hope of becoming close to them, and it hurt me more than I thought it would. Already I yearned for friends, after one day! I never got to say good-bye to my friends back home, few though they were.

We spoke a little about home, eating servings of sandwiches at lunch, but soon they excused themselves to their rooms and left me on my own. Dinner was placed at my door: cold meats and potatoes. I had nothing but my thoughts for company, and I must admit I shed a few tears as the lonely hours wore on.

With time to think, I imagine it is my education that sets me apart from the other commoners. They speak in a rough manner, and they told me they were from the poorer parts of Corcillum and Boreas—not surprising, given their accents. My parents had spared no expense to make me literate and well-spoken, hoping that some-day I might become a lawyer.

Those hopes are now dashed, but the sacrifices my parents made to prepare me as a scholar will serve me well in the days to come. I just hope that these commoners will accept me in time.

Day 4

I have a demon! Sable is my pride and joy, a large beetle of sorts that I am told is called a Mite. She has a black carapace, with a stinger on her tail and mandibles at her mouth. I have not tired of playing with her, for she flits to and fro around my head, as if she cannot tire of looking at me.

Would it be strange to say I already love her? Perhaps it is our con-nected consciousness that makes me care for her so.

She was gifted to me by the provost, the head of Vocans himself! I was taken, along with the others common students, to Lord Scipio's office, where we were each handed a scroll to read from. Juno, Valentine and Tobias struggled to read the strange letters inscribed on the parch-ment, but I spoke them aloud clearly, as instructed, and I confess with not a hint of pride.

It is hard to describe what followed. A drunken sensation, like after I drank the mulled wine my mother allowed me in the dead of last win-ter. And a glowing orb, forming as if from nothingness in front of me, accompanied by a roar louder than a waterfall's bottom. The orb went on spinning and growing, then disappeared in a flash. In its place, my darling Sable hovered, accompanied by a feeling of such joy as I have never experienced before.

Perhaps I should not have been so eager to show off my schooling, for the others glared at me with a vehemence. Yet in that moment, I did not care. I was too happy.

The others also received Mites, smaller ones, but brighter in color—Juno's yellow, Valentine's a deep red and Tobias's a deep blue. They made snide comments about my demon's appearance as Scipio led us back to our rooms, muttered loud enough to hear but too quiet to comment on.

But comment Scipio did. He said drab-colored Mites were the most desired, for they could go unseen at night and were less conspicuous even in the day. The commoners' hatred for me seemed to deepen even further then; I could feel it like the charge in the air before a storm.

It didn't matter. I had a new friend now. Sable.

Day 5

Spells. I cannot say I had pictured spells as something taught before I became a summoner, yet there I was, standing in the center of Vocans's atrium, attempting to "etch" a "glyph" in the air with my fingers. It is not easy—I cannot say I succeeded on the first try, nor indeed after many hours of concentration. The others fared no better. It was only toward the end of the day that I even succeeded in scratching a simple, glowing blue line in the air, before it fizzled out of existence.

Again, the other commoners stared at me jealously when I succeeded before them. I had wished there were nobles there to give them someone else to hate, but we were told that morning that the noble summoners were holidaying in nearby Corcillum—they were too far ahead of us in learning to bother to join our lessons.

As our attention spans dwindled at the lack of success, our teacher, a tousle-haired brunette named Lady Sinclair, took a break to tell us more about demons. It was strange, the four of us sitting on the floor in the great empty space, while she strode back and forth, lecturing.

There are two forms of energy within demons: mana and demonic energy. When we summon a demon and bond it to our essence, their demonic energy fills us. The amount we can absorb varies from summoner to summoner and determines the number of demons that can bond with us. This is known as the fulfilment level.

Generally, more powerful demons have higher levels of demonic energy, so it will be an important determinant of my future prospects. I eagerly await to discover what mine is. Another demon like Sable would be a dream come true!

As the light from the skylight faded, Lady Sinclair informed us that mana was the "fuel" we used for spellcraft. It slowly replenished over time, varying from demon to demon in recovery speed and the amount within them. She told us to picture it as if every demon contained a jar of glowing blue liquid, with a dripping faucet above. Every jar was a different size, and every faucet flowed at a different speed. When we used a spell, the jar would slowly empty. Then it would need the faucet to refill it, until it was full once again.

She also told us that generally, low-level demons such as Sable had smaller jars but faster faucets. High-level demons had larger jars but slower faucets. But this was just a rough rule of thumb.

At this point, servants scurried around us, lighting torches. Frustrated by our failures, or perhaps simply the confused faces of the other commoners, Lady Sinclair gave up on teaching us how to "etch." So, instead we were told to produce the easiest of spells— the wyrdlight. A ball of raw mana that floated aimlessly if not controlled with the summoner's mind, disappearing on contact with anything but air.

This seemed a far easier task, but this time I held back, pretending to struggle until Valentine succeeded in producing his own, a small ball of glowing blue light that drifted around the room, as if a firefly had entered through a keyhole in the wooden doors behind us.

I had hoped that my feigned incompetence would endear me to the others, but they only smirked at me as each succeeded with their own wyrdlights. I don't know why it made me so angry. As I write, I feel only regret.

Because, sick of their scorn, I closed my eyes. Grasping the cord that connected my consciousness to Sable, I channeled the mana into my body until it burned like icy fire through my veins. I pushed it out of my finger, as Lady Sinclair had instructed. The anger helped, I think, because when I opened my eyes a great ball of wyrdlight had formed in the air in front of me, growing larger with each pulse of mana, like a child blowing bubbles through a small hoop.

Then, as it detached from my finger and spun across the room, I instinctively knew how to guide it, nudging it with my mind until it ricocheted into Valentine. Of course, it winked out of existence as soon as it touched him, but his screech of fear as it approached him was satisfying, at least at the time.

Juno tittered at his outburst, and the glare of anger I received from Valentine was almost worth it. Almost.

We walked in silence to our rooms, and Valentine slammed the door behind him, much to the amusement of Juno and Tobias.

Tonight I will not cry. Instead I will practice with wyrdlights, and exercise Sable by having her chase them.

Day 6

I could not produce any more wyrdlights last night. I realize now I had used all my mana in that single, giant wyrdlight, so instead I cuddled Sable to my chest. She is not fluffy or cozy like the house cat we bought last year to keep mice from our bakery. But she is mine, and the love she feels for me burns hotter than the warmest hearth.

But I digress. Today was a day of crushing disappointment.

This morning we were taken to a room in one of the towers. Inside, we were confronted by a giant, segmented pillar made up of multicolored jewels. A "fulfilmeter," one that would determine our fulfilment level and thus, how many demons we could summon. One by one, we were each told to press our hands to it. I was first, and to begin I felt what little mana I had recovered the night before pulled out of me. Then I could feel a new sensation pulsed into me, hot and caustic. A sensation of fullness assailed my senses, and in front, I saw the first segment light up, as if a torch had been lit within. Then another. Finally, a third flickered on and off, until the teacher who had taken us there, a recent graduate called Connor Cavendish, pulled me from the pillar.

"Level three," he told me, and the look of pity in his eyes made my stomach twist. "Just barely."

Was that good? I thought.

Of course, now I know it is not.

Valentine was level six, while Tobias and Juno were level five.

They laughed at me openly, and to his credit, Connor shut them up with a barked order. He told them that with regular practice of spellcraft and demonic control, a summoner might increase their summoning level over time. Also that summoners often grew in fulfilment level naturally as the years went by, though it was different for each summoner. Only time would tell, but hope was not lost.

Then we were done for the day, and I was left to seethe.

As I write this, I try to tell myself that being level three means I can summon two more Mites. That, in itself, is amazing.

But I cannot help but fear for my future. A weak summoner such as myself would have no hope of becoming anything more than a second lieutenant in the army. Worse still, I fear for my own safety, and that of Sable.

You see, in two years' time, I will fight in a grand tournament, the result of which will determine my rank in the army. Noble houses will have the right to offer me a place in their private forces, while the generals of Hominum's military would observe our performance and offer us commissions.

The low-ranked officers fought on the front lines, led men into battle, while the higher ranks sat in warm tents and moved wooden figures around maps, sending soldiers to their deaths. I knew which I would prefer.

It is cold, and the candle runs low. I have no mana for a wyrdlight; the fulfilmeter has taken all of it. And my hopes with it.

Day 7

No. I shall not despair. I am better than the other commoners. I can work harder than them, fight smarter than them. I may never beat the noble summoners, whoever they are. But if these three brats shall be my rivals, then so be it. I need only beat them in the tournament. I write this as I wake. More later tonight.

. . .

Today was a day of rest. So while the others slept and relaxed, I got to work. There is a library here—I learned this from Lord Cavendish, the same teacher who had told the other commoners off for laughing at me and had given me some semblance of hope that I might become a more powerful summoner someday.

He has taken pity on me, and his advice was gratefully received. It seems I reminded him of his younger brother, who had been lucky enough to also inherit the ability to summon (I am told that only the firstborn children of summoners will be guaranteed to inherit the ability—the siblings have a far smaller chance). Connor's brother, Rufus, was still a few years off from attending Vocans, but I was small for my age and we shared the same mousy hair and upturned nose, or so Lord Cavendish said.

Yesterday, I had heard Valentine and the others gossiping about Lord Cavendish. His father was a commoner, and his mother had married his father in disgrace. Later, his mother had disappeared when her flying mount went down somewhere deep in the orc jungles. Valentine said it was fate's way of punishing her for marrying so far below her station. As a commoner himself, I could not understand why he thought this could be true.

In any case, I thanked Lord Cavendish for his direction and went to the library, a great room filled with long benches, armchairs and of course, shelves upon shelves of books. The librarian is called Dame Fairhaven. I like her. She has given me a long list of books to study and help me prepare for the tournament. But she also warned me that book learning will only get me so far.

"If you wanted to become a horse racer, you could study horses and riding until the cows come home," she said, "but you'd never become any good unless you practiced riding the damned things."

Duly noted, Dame Fairhaven. I thank you.

Day 8

I met the first-year nobles today. Well, I say "met." More like I saw them. They do not speak to us; many would not even deign to look at us. They sat at a separate table, so there was not much more to discover. What I do know is there are four of them, two girls and two boys.

I also saw some second-year students, but they kept even farther apart from us than the first-year nobles did. There were commoners among them too, but I rarely saw them, even in the commoners' quarters. When I did, I never received anything more than a polite nod.

Summoning was the first lesson together with the nobles, and I am pleased to see that it is being taught by the closest person I have to a friend (forgetting Sable of course), Lord Cavendish. Even so, it was a terrifying affair. We learned to "infuse" our demons and then summon them back into existence. Infusion required placing our demons in the center of a pentacle—a five-pointed star surrounded by a circle. This pentacle had to be made out of organic material too, so we were given "summoning leathers," an essential part of a summoner's tool kit. Mine was little larger than a handkerchief, since Sable is so small. Some of the nobles had quiver-like cylinders on their backs with their larger leathers in them.

Apparently, a giant demon could be infused even using a summoner leather as small as mine, but it was harder to do. The larger the demon and the smaller the pentacle, the harder it was to infuse them.

I still remember that moment when I first infused Sable. The nobles just watched, their demons either absent or hidden within them. I think

they were sizing up the competition. After all, in two years, we would face one another.

I placed Sable on the mat and concentrated, doing as instructed by Lord Cavendish. Kneeling, I placed my hand on the mat's edge and pushed mana into the pentacle, until I felt an obstacle between Sable's consciousness and my own. Then, as the pentacle fizzled, giving off the acrid stench of burning leather, I drew Sable's essence through and she dissolved into threads of white light. Then she was inside me, and my body was suffused with an unnatural euphoria. It was so intense that I fell on my side and twitched until it passed.

To my surprise, and perhaps selfish disappointment, Valentine, Tobias and Juno all succeeded in doing the same. I heard a muttered comment from one of the nobles—that it was easier to infuse pathetic demons such as Sable. That his demon would crush our Mites to a paste in the tournament.

Later, I caught his name and marked him as one to watch out for. Jamie Fitzroy.

Day 9

I have a new tutor—the weapons master of Vocans. They call him Sir Caulder. A grizzled man, missing one arm and one leg, but as wily and agile as a man half his age. He was curious to learn where we had come from, asking us each in turn our age and upbringing.

The nobles did not attend his lessons, which took place in the evenings, when they would rather be carousing in Corcillum. Not to mention that most of them had private weapons tutors.

Our lessons took place in the arena, a place I was told would someday be where I faced my peers in the tournament. It was a sandy circle, with seat-stepping in concentric rings around it. The corridor into the arena had been lined with barred cells—built a few years back for deserters, or captured orcs. They had almost never been used. Even the few gremlins that had been captured were too small for the cages. I recently learned that gremlins are a servile species long since enslaved to the orcs, if the books I have been reading are accurate.

In any case, Sir Caulder has started me on training to fight with a straight sword. Each of us has been given a cutting weapon—Valentine a saber, Tobias an axe and Juno a cutlass.

We will train with him each week—though I have already asked for extra lessons. While the others joke and chatter each evening, becoming fast friends, I shall be down here, perfecting my swordcraft. I am shorter than them, and chubbier too—my mother always said customers liked a rosy-cheeked baker's boy to deliver their bread.

But that will soon change. If I am to become a leader of men, then they will need a lean wolf in their midst—not a plump lamb ready for slaughter.

Day 10

Demonology. I love demonology, even if I dislike our teacher, Lord Etherington, with a venom that would almost feel irrational if he wasn't such a git. This time, the nobles joined us. They even paid attention. I think it was out of respect for our teacher more than a desire to learn though.

He is a fearsome man, tall and bearlike with a black beard that comes down to his waist. But behind the fierce exterior is a shrewd, even cunning man, whose sharp tongue cut each commoner to the core as he asked us questions that of course none of us knew the answers to.

Lord Etherington seemed to take pleasure in making us feel like fools. Even when I answered the first question correctly (thanks to my studying in the library last night), he followed up with another. What happens to a demon when its summoner dies? I did not know, and the tongue lashing I received at my unpreparedness near brought me to tears.

He explained in withering tones that an "untethered" demon will fade back into the ether—whence it came from.

Luckily, the sniggering from Valentine, the nobles and the others turned Lord Etherington's attention to them. Five minutes later and they were as cowed as I was.

Yet, when the nobles did not know the answers to his questions, he did not treat them in the same way. Of course, my father warned me to expect such bigotry here, but it did not make the foul taste it left in my mouth any more palatable.

I remained with my head down for the rest of the lesson, but I ate up every word from that vile man's mouth and was amazed by his sketches and charts. I will be sure to hunt down some demonology treatises from the library later. I shall not allow myself to be caught out again.

Day 12

I am finding it harder and harder to keep up with you, dear journal. With my additional studies, it is difficult to find the time to write down what I already know, and I confess, it can be painful to relive each day of loneliness and disappointment. Yesterday, when the others were resting, I studied in the library. But the texts are ancient and hard to understand, written for noble, expert summoners, not common novices such as I. Still, I shall persevere where I can.

Today we studied spellcraft once more. It seems that there are as many as thousands of spells to master, but given our war with the orcs, we focus on a few key battle spells to learn. There are even rumors of the first-year graduates being sent to the front lines early.

More depressing still, I am no longer the best at spellcraft. Valentine performed a fire spell before I was able to, and he did not let me forget it. Of course, the nobles were well ahead of us, scoffing at the small ball of flame that we all eventually managed to bring into existence.

I shall have to practice more.

Day 15

It was our second summoning lesson today. Lord Cavendish did not return my smile when I entered the room. Does he still care for me? Or is he taking care not to show favoritism?

I should not let it get to me. How pathetic am I, to seek the pity of my teachers?

In any case, this time, the nobles did not bother to show up for class. Lord Cavendish explained that the first lessons would be going over things that many of the nobles already knew. He sounded quite defensive, in my opinion, and disappointed in his small class of four.

First, we were shown how to "scry." We commoners were told to pay particular attention, for our Mites are the species that summoners scry with the most. It was simple enough. We were each given a shard of flat crystal, which we tapped against our demons' carapaces.

When we did so, an image formed on the crystal, showing everything that our Mites could see from then on. Stranger still, there was an odd echo in my mind. It turns out that you can hear everything your demon does when it has been connected to a scrying crystal and said crystal is held in your hand. Giving the crystal to another summoner does not allow them to also hear though.

The rest was quite simple—cajoling our demons with our minds to move around the room. Lord Cavendish told us it was important to exercise demonic control, especially from long distances. It was easy really, not unlike moving a wyrdlight.

But all that changed when we were told to send our demons out of the summoning room and into the atrium, where Lord Cavendish had hung several hoops from the balconies. Without sight of Sable, it was far harder to control her direction.

Eventually, we learned that the best way to control our demons when out of sight was to see their movements with the crystal and impress on them our desires, indicating our intentions down the mental cord that held our consciousnesses together.

I was not good at demonic control. Tonight, I shall improve upon it.

Day 16

Each morning, I have gone down to the baths for my morning ablutions and checked my plump body in the mirror. I am still that baker's boy, cherubic-faced and looking much younger than my true age. The only difference so far is the dark circles under my eyes, which are bloodshot from squinting at illegible scrawls in centuries-old books.

I am eating less, though whether it is a lack of appetite from the sadness I feel or my desire to gain a warrior's physique I cannot say. Only Sable keeps me company, but she can only do so much.

Weapons training is exhausting work, but I gloried in the sweat that dripped from me at the end of the session, even if Juno pinched her nose and muttered that I stank of stale bacon. I can tell Sir Caulder is impressed with my enthusiasm, even if I did flail my wooden sword with an exuberance that made him chuckle on occasion.

Day 22

I have neglected you, dear journal, but there has not been much to say this past week. I studied, I practiced and I improved in all things summoning. I devoured my demonology lessons and even earned a grunt of approval from Lord Etherington.

There is much to say today though.

My life changed. Of course, by now I had heard of the "ether," the other dimension where our demons come from. I had learned of their food chains, their habits, their mana levels and other things.

But seeing is believing.

Lord Cavendish wheeled out a table at the start of our lesson today, one made of the purest white marble with a dark, oval crystal in its center. Then he told us it was the "Oculus," the largest scrying crystal ever found. The crystal type, known as corundum, was incredibly rare. That was why our scrying crystals were small shards, while those of the nobles were far larger, some even embedded in what might have been hand mirrors.

He placed his Damsel upon there, a demon that looked not unlike a

giant dragonfly, and then chose one of the pentacles arrayed across the leather floor of the room. The pentacle he selected was larger than the others, but strangest of all, it had a series of symbols around its edge.

These, we were told, were "keys." Coordinates to an approximate location in the ether, where Hominum's summoners hunted for new demons to add to their rosters.

He embedded a leather rope into the pentacle's edge and powered it by pulsing mana into the pattern. Soon, the pentacle and its keys glowed and the same glowing orb that had formed when I first summoned Sable appeared above it . . . only larger.

Then, without warning, his Damsel disappeared into the orb with a buzz of its wings.

Within the Oculus, the world turned red. It was a desert of dust and pillars of stone, with whirlwinds drifting across the plain. I wondered, how could it be that Sable lived in this wasteland?

It was then that Lord Cavendish told us that we were on the outer edge of the ether. The ether is disk shaped, you see. I included a diagram based on his descriptions below.

Lord Cavendish was scared—the "keys" are inaccurate things, and his demon had appeared far closer to the ether's rim than he would have liked. Still, he told us to keep watching and sent his demon toward the ground, but not before we saw the edge itself—a broad cliff that stretched seemingly endlessly to the left and right, with the barest discernible curve to it indicating just how enormous the ether must be.

Beyond the drop-off was an abyss so black that it almost hurt to look at.

He next sent his demon crawling to the edge, so slowly that my legs even began to ache from standing still. But finally, his demon reached the precipice and gazed out into the darkness.

What I saw there made my stomach twist with horror. Deep in the void, somewhere far below, monsters lurked. No two looked alike, though it was hard to tell in that writhing mass of tentacles, eyes and teeth.

The Damsel looked for no more than a few seconds before beginning its long crawl back. It was a while before he allowed the demon to take flight once more, heading away from the monsters, or Ceteans, as I later learned they were called.

He was sweating by the time the scenery changed, the terror of the Ceteans and the constant expenditure of mana taking their toll. But soon I forgot all about him, because I was staring into green jungle. Above, flocks and swarms of demons swirled across the horizon, while beyond, pillars of smoke from volcanoes broke up the sky.

The Damsel was quick to enter the foliage though, where beneath, the mulch of rotten leaves and rich black soil made up the jungle floor. There, I could see more demons flying to and fro, mostly lesser Mites and other Damsels. But there were other demons there, too many to name now, but each one more fascinating than the last.

Lord Cavendish only remained for five minutes in that viridescent jungle, but each minute felt like a lifetime. I wanted to go there and said as much. It was only later that I would learn that the air in the ether is poisonous to humans, and that only those wearing a special airtight suit with an air pipe going back into the portal can enter, and even then, only for a brief time.

Still, I left the lesson feeling invigorated. I could not wait to send Sable into her old world and bring back a new Mite friend, or perhaps even a Damsel.

Day 25

I went exploring today. Valentine and the others have made it their mission to ignore me, it seems. They do not like that I study so much, or that I stay after training to receive private tutoring from Sir Caulder. They themselves are too lazy, and since they won't speak to me, my only other alternative is to stare at the wall of my room all day. They only have themselves to blame.

But I cannot stand another day in that stuffy library, and my mana is so low from practice that I fear I will not recover enough for spellcraft lessons tomorrow. So, I decided to wander the corridors of Vocans.

I have found myself particularly drawn to the strange jars of pickled demons that appear at intervals along the walls here. That, and the orcish weapons and occasional painted sections of orcish runes, scrawled on hunks of peeled bark or primitive papyrus.

Once, this was a place of learning and curiosity. Now, there is only war.

I befriended a servant in my wanderings. He is young, perhaps twelve years old, but we struck up a lively enough conversation discussing an enormous pickled demon, one that had been labeled "Cockatrice." Of course, the brine that surrounded it within the jar had stripped it of its coloring, but one could still see the smattering of feathers and scales that had once adorned its body, with its strange lizard tail and cockerel's beak and talons that made it a sight to behold.

It was then that this boy, Jeffrey, imparted a secret to me. Most of these specimens had come from a room in the northwest tower. He often delivered food there, and the most impressive specimens could be found inside. Giving me no more information than that, he led me there, pausing only to admire a painting.

In the background, dwarven women had their veils ripped away by human onlookers, while in the foreground, dwarven warriors kneeled in rows, their beards being cut by men in armor. Corpses of the fallen dwarves surrounded them, and above, summoners flew on their demons with bloodied lances.

"Just as it should be," was all the boy said, then carried on toward the tower.

I knew very little of the dwarves. Of course I have seen them before, but they live apart from us—their lives are a mystery. Still, the hatred in the boy's voice sent a shudder down my spine, and I resolved that perhaps he would not be my friend for long.

When we reached the tower, Jeffrey unlocked an unusual room that took up what must have been the entirety of the turret and showed me in.

What was inside set my curiosity ablaze. All around, pickled demons gazed silently back at me, many missing limbs and organs. Fat candles sat beneath beakers and jars of bubbling liquid, while strange charts and symbols adorned the walls.

I felt a hand fall upon my shoulder. I must confess, I let out an unmanly yelp of fear. It was then that I met Electra Mabosi.

The servant, Jeffrey, was dismissed forthwith, but I was told to remain. I trembled as she observed me, and in turn I observed her back. She clearly hailed from the land of Swazulu across the Vesanian Sea, for her skin was far darker than my own and her head was capped with short curls. She wore a white-cloth coat, and her hands were clad in thick leather gloves that were covered in disgusting stains.

I do not remember the exact wording of our conversation. But it was something like this:

"Curiosity is to be encouraged," she said. "Snooping is not."

"I wasn't snooping! Jeffrey brought me here. I just wanted to see more demons."

She looked at me strangely then. She tapped her chin with a glove, leaving a yellow stain streaked across her chin. I shuddered.

"I need someone like you. Someone with curiosity. I have heard reports from Lord Etherington—you're a good student."

"He said that?" I asked.

She ignored me.

"Before, I would ask graduates to work for me. But who wants to keep studying once they've graduated? They just want to go off and fight in their wars, order their soldiers about."

I didn't understand, but I remained silent. She could still get me into trouble, if she wanted to.

"But you . . . maybe you're the one. And you can't run off and fight a war if you haven't graduated yet. Yes. . . ."

She pulled up a chair and sat opposite me.

"Are you brave, James?"

I nodded, and she smiled.

"Lord Etherington and I have been working on a secret project. Do you know what keys are?"

"Yes, they're coordinates to the ether."

"To a certain part of the ether," she corrected me. "Well, did you know that the orcs use a different set of keys?"

I shook my head.

"You see, the orcs capture their demons in an entirely different part of the ether. That's why orcs often use different demons to our own. We tend to use demons that are native to our part of the ether—Canids, Felids and the like. They tend to use demons such as Nanaues and Sobeks."

I nodded once more. It made sense—a different ecosystem meant different demons.

"So you see, we need to find the keys to their part of the ether. Can you imagine the knowledge we could discover there? New demons, new spells. It could change the course of the war."

"Spells?" I asked.

Electra smiled at me.

"Certain demons have abilities that use mana. For example, the Phoenix can breathe fire. But did you know that the reason it is able to do this is that it has a fire symbol inside its throat? Long ago, the earliest summoners dissected dead demons to find the symbols inside them, which are the spells we use today. If we were to do the same with orc demons . . . well . . . think of the new spells we could discover."

It was a lot to take in. But now I understood the dead demons floating in jars.

"We could fight the orcs in their part of the ether, prevent their shamans from capturing new demons for their army. And we could start capturing new varieties of demons for our own army. This is important, James. And you could help me do it."

"How?" I asked, shuddering involuntarily. What could I possibly do to help?

"Now, you run along back to your room. I'll have work for you soon enough," Electra said, giving me a crazed smile. She led me to the doors and propelled me out.

And I admit, when she shut the doors behind me . . . I ran.

Day 31

As the days go by, I begin to see more demons. The nobles have begun to show theirs off, but now I see that Electra was right. There is little variety in the species these nobles use—mostly Canids and Felids as she described. I yearn to see others in the flesh, the same ones that Lord Etherington shows us in his lessons.

Speaking of Lord Etherington, he has begun to treat me better than the others. I believe Electra has spoken to him about me. But I dread to think what plans they have for me.

Day 47

I saw the beginnings of muscle on my stomach today. If I shine a wyrd-light directly above me anyway. The pudgy flesh around my cheeks has given way, and I no longer feel the weight of my stomach on my knees when I bend over to tie my laces.

Did a servant girl smile at me the other day, or was it at Jamie Fitzroy behind me? In any case . . . I shall continue my training and studies. Only two rashers of bacon for me tomorrow, instead of the usual four.

Day 48

I saw the servant girl canoodling with Fitzroy today. Damn.

Day 57

As I study more and more, I am beginning to see the importance of the elves. They were the first summoners, and though they lost the ability to summon centuries ago, it would seem that they knew more about summoning then than we do now.

Dame Fairhaven has taken pity on me and has given me a treatise on the elves. I have copied it down here, in the hopes that it gives me some clues to discovering new keys.

Millennia ago, they imparted the ability to summon to King Corwin and his nobles. I wonder . . . did the elves use the same keys as we use now? More study is needed.

As I write this, Sable is tugging on my sleeve, eager to play. So, I end the entry here.

TREATISE ON THE ELVES
By Lord Edmund Raleigh

Trade between the elves and the people of Hominum has been my life's work. Resistance has been strong on both sides, a consequence of distrust and suspicion sown by old rivalries and past transgressions. Some progress has been made, but I fear I have failed in my demands. Even so, I have formed good friendships with some of their clan leaders, and I hope that my descendants will succeed where I have failed.

In my time visiting the elves, I have learned a great deal about their history and culture. This, I impart to the scriptures of Vocans now, in the hopes that it will serve for better understanding between our species.

Elves have existed in what is known as the Great Forest for millennia. There, they live in the treetops themselves, making their homes in carved hollows of the trunks and passing between them using living bridges of twisted root, vine and branch.

They are far longer lived than we are, capable of reaching two hundred years of age. However, elves reach adulthood at the same time as us, and generally share the same maturity. It is only their middle age that lasts far longer than our own.

The species is segregated into clans with their own chieftains, much like the noble houses that we have in Hominum. However, there is no single ruler, but instead a council of chieftains that votes on matters of law and state. War between clans is extremely rare, but dueling between chieftains and their families was once commonplace. Such violence became so widespread and deadly that summoning was banned for four hundred years. The ability to summon has now been lost to the elves.

This is an irony not lost upon them, as it was the elves who first taught King Corwin and our other noble ancestors how to summon in the first place, in exchange for driving the orcs back into their jungles. It is their fervent hope to bring back summoning, especially considering that the majority of elves are born as level seven summoners, far higher than our human average.

I am told that their libraries are full of knowledge that far surpasses our own: ancient texts that give deep insight into new spells, the ether's geography, its demons and their abilities. There is certainly the opportunity to trade for such knowledge in the future, but they are reluctant to do so without summoners of their own. It is an ongoing discussion.

Elves are also formed of two distinct castes, between which intermarriage and breeding is strictly prohibited, on pain of banishment.

It is the high elves who hold power in the Great Forest, serving in the roles of academics and other learned trades. Elven doctors are some of the best in the world, with medicines that we can only dream of. It is my hope that we will someday be able to acquire some of these medicines, but it is hard to speak to the high elves at the best of times. This caste spends most of their time in the trees, and it is not unheard of for some to never set foot on the ground their entire lives.

The wood elves live on the forest floor, tending the Great Herds. These herds are made up of thousands of deer, with dozens of different species living together. These provide the elves with much of their resources, resources that Hominum is very much in need of. These include furs and leathers for clothing and blankets, meat and milk for our tables, bones and antlers for carving, sinews and rawhide for bowstrings and stitching, and fats for tallow, soaps, candles and glues.

This caste is considered to be closer to nature, and it is not unheard of for them to keep birds as pets, as well as foxes and other such creatures to help them corral and protect the herds. Wood elves differ in appearance to high elves. The latter are always pale and blond, with blue eyes, while the former tend to have darker hair and eyes of hazel. Both castes share long, pointed ears and dark rings around their irises, and are generally considered to be stronger and more athletic than humans are to varying degrees.

All elves have an affinity to the bow, though wood elves seem to surpass their high elf cousins in that regard. Both use similar garments and weapons when going into battle: lamellar armor of vivid colors and large, two-handed falx swords. It is not uncommon for elves to fight mounted upon elk or moose, making for a deadly cavalry that Hominum cannot match.

Finally, I must confess to a millennia-old legend that I have heard whispers of in my travels there. It tells of a third caste—known as the dark elves. The story goes that these red-eyed, black-haired elves lived beneath the ground, in among the roots of the trees. This caste was said to have been banished south long ago, when it was discovered that they were performing necromancy. It is said that they perverted the use of demonic energy to bring corpses back from the dead to serve as their undead servants, killing their demons in the process. Supposedly, nothing has been heard of them since.

Day 73

Today, Lord Etherington took me aside after our demonology lesson. I had hoped that Electra had forgotten about me, but alas, it seems she has found something for me to do. Still, Lord Etherington was so kind as to offer me a trip to Corcillum tomorrow. I have accepted. After almost three months of being cooped up in this castle, I'd go to the orc jungles themselves for a change of scenery.

Day 74

Our carriage ride to Corcillum was . . . an awkward affair. Lord Etherington did not say much. In truth, he arranged our carriage so early that even the servants were not up. He kept glancing about as he urged me into the carriage and then stared nervously out the window until Vocans was out of sight.

I write in my diary now, to fill the silence as we judder along the cobbles. It seems he is scared of the carriage driver overhearing us—he is a servant at Vocans.

If I had to guess, my involvement in whatever plans he and Electra have devised for me have not been sanctioned by Provost Scipio. Still, if it helps me advance in this world, I shall follow this where it leads. It's research after all. How dangerous can it be?

The carriage has stopped. More soon.

We went to the Anvil Tavern. It is a place for dwarven sympathizers and dwarves and is not frequented by nobles. Perhaps that is why Lord Etherington took me there—for fear of being seen elsewhere.

It was strange to see so many dwarves in one place. They stared at us suspiciously over their meals, and my stomach rumbled at the sight of the fried root vegetables and dumplings they were eating. I had missed breakfast.

The tavern was nearly empty, it being so early in the morning, but Lord Etherington bought me a large tankard of beer, and I supped it as we spoke. I was a little tipsy by the end of our conversation, drinking on an empty stomach and all, and it tasted sour to my unaccustomed tongue.

Perhaps it was the beer that made me accept his offer so readily. But now, in the cold light of the morning, with my head aching from the beer I drank, I wonder if it was the right choice.

He said he would help me advance at Vocans. That I might even graduate early, if I played my cards right, and serve as an officer in his own regiment. All I needed to do was work hard, and he would do the rest.

Even in my drunken state, I probed him, indirectly, to try to find out the cause for all this secrecy. And so he told me, in a roundabout way.

The orcs were the problem. Studying them was banned among the nobility—their savagery was not to be emulated. Their ways were old and archaic. Even believing that the orcs used a different set of keys was rarely spoken about. Speculating that they might know something we didn't was considered treasonous talk, and grounds for demotion in the army, as well as being made a laughingstock among the nobility.

Now, Electra cared little for what other people thought, but she was scared of the outdoors—it had been years since she had left her chamber, let alone the Vocans grounds. She would not venture into the jungles and study their villages, their remains, their ways. It was hard enough convincing soldiers to bring her the corpses of orcish demons—only Lord Etherington's regiment did so, and he kept them out of the thick of the fighting.

But . . . a student, and a commoner no less. Such a person could study the orcs, in plain sight. They could ignore the jibes, endure the loss in reputation. Basically, I wasn't important enough for anyone to care what I thought.

Then he told me matter-of-factly what my future would hold, should I not accept his offer. He predicted I would spend two miserable years at Vocans, where the other students would far outstrip me in all things, beating me through sheer power, no matter how hard I trained.

With such a low summoning level, at the end of those two years I could expect to be drafted into the army as a second lieutenant, the lowest rank. Then I would be thrown against the orcs in battle after battle, until I was expended. Such was the fate of common summoners—or at least low-level ones.

If I accepted Lord Etherington's offer, he would keep me safe. I would be his eyes and ears, learning all I could about the shamans and their demons. And we would share the credit when I eventually succeeded.

I asked him how I could graduate after just one year . . . surely I had to wait for the tournament. He told me to let him worry about that.

So I agreed, slurring my words slightly. He gave me fare for the carriage ride back and more besides, then he left me. And what a day I had—let me tell you.

Or rather, I won't, because I am exhausted. Tomorrow, then.

Day 75

So, there I was in the dwarfish tavern, staring at more silver than my father earned in a month. Lord Etherington had handed it to me as if it were nothing.

I closed my hand around it, but not before a few of the dwarves saw.

I worried then. Dwarves are always being arrested—they fill our jails to overflowing.

So when one sidled up to me, I gulped down the last of my beer and stood to leave. I quietly cursed my decision to infuse Sable earlier, even if it had been at Lord Etherington's request.

The dwarf held up his hands placatingly.

"Your father likes our beer, I see," he said.

Then I knew I was safe. A dwarf was taking his life into his own hands if he robbed a noble-born. I didn't correct him. I think the conversation went something like this—though my memory was fuddled by the beer.

"My name is Athol," he said. "And I see you don't carry a blade as the other nobles do. Perhaps you are in need of one?"

A blade. My heart quickened at the thought. I had seen the swords that Sir Caulder kept in the arena—though we had not been allowed to practice with them yet (only wooden replicas). Rusted things, made from pig iron and heavy as lead. To have my own sword . . .

"Perhaps," I allowed.

"I am but an apprentice, but I have some weapons that might be to your liking. May I show you?"

I acquiesced, and together we left the tavern.

He led me to a back alley. It was rather stupid of me to follow him into the darkness, now that I think about it, but luck was on my side that day. He removed his backpack—an enormous thing that came down to his knees—and unrolled a long cloth from inside.

Within were a dozen blades, each more magnificent than the last, or at least, to my untrained eyes.

"They're simple things—I'm not trained in engraving yet. But they've a fine balance and edge."

So I could see. I knew that eventually I would fight with a real blade against my fellow students. A good blade would give me an edge—if you'll pardon the pun, dear journal.

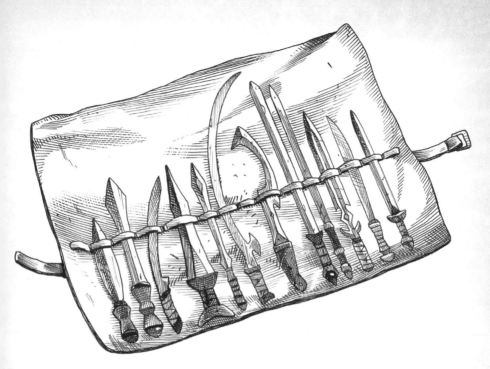

"What are you looking for?" Athol asked me.

What indeed?

I knew one thing—in the tournament, our bodies were protected by a barrier spell. The blades could bruise, but not cut. So sharpness was not a thing I needed. But balance and speed were.

"What do the other nobles use?" I asked.

Athol smiled at that. I realized then, he already knew I was not a noble—my accent would have given it away as soon as I opened my mouth. Not to mention my uniform was clearly secondhand.

"They use rapiers," he replied. "Fast fencing blades, no edge, made for scoring points in your tournament. Useless against orcs, mind you."

I grimaced at that. I didn't want to buy and practice with a blade that would eventually be useless. He caught my expression. I think he took pity on me then.

"Nobles have training, you see. You won't beat them at their own game. And you're short—they'll have a longer reach than you."

"So what should I do?" I asked.

"You won't be as fast. But you can be stronger than them. I reckon you need a heavy blade—something that can beat their thin stabbing swords aside and let you get in close. Not too short—they'll dance back before you can hit them. But not too long either—you need to chop down quick."

He lifted my arm from its side and took in my measurements with a glance.

"You'll be wanting a spatha. King Corwin's weapon of choice, a classic. Good for fighting orcs, good for fencing. You can't go wrong."

He pointed to a straight blade with a sharp point, as long as my arm. Its hilt was a basic rectangle of wood, and the grip was made of bound leather. But it gleamed in the dull morning light, and I knew I had to have it.

He lifted it and balanced it on his finger in its center. It hung perfectly.

"Dwarven steel. Balanced, sharp. Heavy enough to knock a rapier askew, light enough to maneuver."

I wanted it more with every word.

"How much?" I asked.

"Twenty shillings," came the swift reply. I looked at the silver still clutched in my palm. It was the exact same amount. Had he counted it in the tavern? It seemed a fair price, from what little I knew.

"I'll tell you what," Athol said, "I'll throw in the scabbard for free."

He tugged forth the sheath from his backpack, a simple, leather-bound thing that would attach to my belt loop easily enough.

"I won't have enough for a ride back to Vocans," I replied.

Athol frowned.

"I can't go lower," he said. "A dwarf has to make a living, you know. This is a fine blade."

So I accepted. And now you know why I was so exhausted yesterday, dear journal.

I walked back.

Day 79

I don't think I could have been more nervous
than when Sir Caulder assessed my new spatha.
Luckily, after a few swishes in the air, he grunted
his approval.

"Did you steal it?" was all he asked. I shook my
head . . . and it was back to training.

The other commoners watched on in jealousy as I
whirled the blade about. I believe I cut quite the dashing
figure, even if Juno rolled her eyes at me when I smiled at
her. Alas, I shall not melt that icy heart just yet.

Training with a spatha is different from training with a
cutlass. Sir Caulder expects me to meet each cut with a parry of
my own instead of dodging, to stab more than I slash. In particular, he has taught me how to get in close—to catch the enemy blade
on my own and press in, then use my strength to overcome them.
Only . . . I don't have the strength just yet. He now has me on a
regime of forty push-ups in my room each night. You shall have to
forgive the sweat marks on your pages today—I have just finished
doing them.

I feel new confidence. That dwarf may have made a profit, but he
was a godsend. I don't care what Jeffrey says. They aren't a bad lot.

Day 80

Demonology lessons were particularly interesting today. We went over
the most common orc demons—Kamaitachis, Nanaues and the like. It
seems our conversation six days ago inspired Lord Etherington. I am
beginning to think I misjudged him.

Is he using me? Perhaps we are using each other.

Day 92

It would seem that Lord Etherington's plan to have me graduate a year early has come to fruition. This morning, at breakfast, Provost Scipio made an announcement.

There would be a "mock tournament" at the end of the year for the first-year students, to help us prepare for the real thing. Lord Etherington had suggested that even a few generals and other summoners attend. And, most importantly, should anyone show real promise, they *might* even earn themselves a commission as an officer.

He said it with a wink and a nudge, not truly serious, but Lord Etherington, who had accompanied him, looked meaningfully at me across the room.

Later, Lord Etherington took me aside, waiting for me near the library.

"There are no guarantees in this," he told me. "If you make a poor showing, it will be suspicious if I offer you a commission. You need to do well."

"How am I supposed to do that?" I asked him.

"By working harder than everyone else. This is first year—the nobles tend to slack off so you might be able to beat one if you're lucky. And the other commoners may have higher summoning levels, but in the first year they'll still only have a Mite, same as you. You have a chance, at least this year. Next year . . . they'll be way ahead of you."

"Can you help me?" I asked. "Maybe some private tutoring?"

"It will arouse suspicion," he replied.

A servant scurried past, barely giving us a second look. But it was enough—Lord Etherington strode off without a word, leaving me alone in the dark corridor.

Day 100

It's hard to imagine I've only been here a hundred days. It feels like so much longer! I miss my parents dearly. I have tried to write to them a dozen times, but the words will not come. How strange that I can pour out my innermost feelings to you, dear journal. I talk to Sable sometimes—and she understands more than I think, even if they are just my emotions. Scarab Mites are intelligent creatures.

Day 125

I wake, I work and I sleep. I have barely found the time to write—more than once, Dame Fairhaven has found me in the library, reading over ancient books. Already I have made much progress in my study of the orcs. There have been summoners before me who have seen a city built around a pyramid so ancient that none know when it was built.

Strangely, Lady Cavendish—Lord Cavendish's mother—has been a useful source. As a member of the Celestial Corps, she had scouted deep into enemy territory on the back of her Peryton and even made sketches of their great city from above. I re-create some of them here.

Of course, it cost her in the end, taking such risks. She was seen going down over the jungles a few years back. Her body was never recovered.

TREATISE ON THE ORCS

by Lord Edmund Raleigh

It seems that my treatise on the elves was so popular that the librarian has requested another from me. So I write all my knowledge of the orcs, in the hopes of educating young minds about our oldest and most dangerous foe.

Living on the borders of their jungles, it seems that I am one of the most qualified to write about them. However, it is important to remember that much of what I know is based on hearsay and word of mouth, rather than firsthand knowledge.

Though we have never captured an orc for study, anecdotal evidence suggests that they age far faster than we do, reaching maturity at the age of ten and living only to fifty years old or thereabouts. At full maturity, bull orcs will grow to the size of seven feet or higher, with prominent tusks in place of their lower canines. Females are smaller in stature and have smaller tusks, but are no less deadly.

Specimens are known to wear a variety of body paints, tattoos, bone armors, feather decorations, animal skins and leaf skirts over their gray skin. Their hairstyles also differ by tribes, ranging from shaven patches to topknots and bowl-shaped mops. Piercings are also not uncommon, usually with bone, ivory or carved wood.

Orc weaponry is almost never metallic, with a focus on clubs and stone axes. Their favored weapon is the macana, a flat club with obsidian shards embedded on the sides. These weapons are in fact sharper than steel, though the edges more brittle, and are capable of decapitating a horse with a single blow.

It is not unheard of for orcs to ride rhinos into battle. These creatures are also raised for their milk, or to transport resources around. Hyenas are also a popular pet for orcs, taking on the role that dogs play in our own culture.

Orcs seem to be split into two separate forms of society. The first is relatively peaceful: small villages made up of a few families living in harmony with the land. Human encounters with these groups are often hostile in nature, but it seems they have almost no male warriors among them, for reasons that will be mentioned below.

The second society is based in their only city, with thousands of orcs gathering there for religious ceremonies, or living on the outskirts in much larger villages. This society is made almost entirely of male warriors, whose numbers are supplemented by the kidnapping of young orcs from the villages mentioned previously. These young males are indoctrinated to become violent religious zealots, and it is this civilization that is at odds with Hominum. Unfortunately, our soldiers cannot tell the difference between the first and second, slaughtering indiscriminately when any orcs are encountered.

The violence of the orcish civilization has been noted by our scouts, who have seen some of the more brutal games that the orcs play among themselves, in part for entertainment, but also to weed out the weak and select victims for their sacrificial rites on the pyramid that dominates the center of their sandstone-built city. The pyramid's origins are unknown, and it has been theorized by ancient elvish academics that it was not in fact built by the orcs. There are also unproven statements from these same scholars that the interior of the pyramid is covered in hieroglyphics, which may or may not be the basis for their religion.

Several of the orcs' religious games are listed below:

PITZ (in honor of the wind god): A ball game designed to get a rubber sphere through a hoop by hitting it with a club. These clubs may also be used against opponents during the game, leaving many of the participants crippled, maimed or dead. The losing team is almost always sacrificed.

VENATIO (in honor of the animal gods): A gladiatorial arena where three individuals are tied together by the ankle and are set upon by wild animals. These animals include hyenas, jaguars, tigers, lions, crocodiles and baboons. There are rarely any survivors, as the dead bodies of their followers hamper those trying to maneuver in the arena.

SKIN-PULL (in honor of the fire god): In which a skin is stretched across a pit full of flames in a tug of war. The opposing teams attempt to pull the other team into the pit.

NAUMCHIA (in honor of the water god): A giant pool of crocodile-infested water is created, while teams of orcs in canoes attempt to overturn the others, using clubs to aid them. It is common for the water to be red with blood by the end of the spectacle. Orc society is stratified by shamans who act as the de facto rulers of the orcs, being both their religious leaders and military commanders. These shamans teach summoning via a system of apprenticeship, with no official schooling. It is not unknown for shamans to travel from village to village, copulating with young females in the hopes of producing more offspring with the ability to summon.

One mystery that is yet to be solved is the fact that orcs regularly summon very different demons to our own, though there is some crossover. These differing species tend to be demons that inhabit oceans and swamps, which we lack in the part of the ether that our own summoners capture demons from. We have also never encountered another portal belonging to a shaman there. This has led some to theorize that the orcs summon from a different part of the ether to us and possess the symbols (or keys) to that location. This is yet to be confirmed.

Finally, it is a well-known fact that albino orcs have some special significance to orc religion and culture. It is suspected that they serve as both a prophet and savior, though this is not to be confirmed. It is said they are taller still than the average orc and have high summoning levels, but these rumors are likely spurious at best.

NB. Some years ago, I was told that the birth of an albino orc had been witnessed by some novice summoners in the jungles. Though I believe them, there has been no sign of it since. It is my fervent, if somewhat morbid hope that the child died soon after birth. Cruel though it may seem, the last time an albino led the orcs, war broke out between our peoples. I can only pray that it does not happen again.

Day 127

I have been found out. Lord Cavendish asked to see me today in his office, after our summoning lesson. I made the mistake of asking him too many questions about the keys—if we could make them more accurate, where they came from, what the symbols mean. I even asked what the orcs use—after all, as Lord Etherington said, my reputation matters not a jot.

But as it turns out, it was not this that aroused his suspicions; it only confirmed them.

"Whatever Lord Etherington has asked you to do, I beg of you, do not do it," he said as soon as I entered the room.

I stuttered a garbled response, but he held up a hand, stopping me.

"I have seen the books and treatises you have been reading in the library. Even for one as inquisitive as you, your area of study is too specific to be mere coincidence."

He seemed angry, though I could not understand why.

"My mother died working for that man. He offered her money. Our family is poor; when she married a commoner, my father, it impoverished our family. And she was a patriot; she believed in his cause. But he asked too much of her. He is a zealot, a fanatic. Trust me when I say this: He will not hesitate to put your life at risk if it helps him get to the truth."

I asked him what other choice I had. I was a low-level commoner— I would be fighting on the front lines regardless. It was *safer* for me this way.

He only shook his head.

"I hope you're right," was all he said. Then he dismissed me.

Day 137

As I study the orcs more and more, I begin to suspect that their coordinates within the ether are near an ocean, and perhaps a swamp. Reading old journals of summoners who battled the orcs in the First Orc War, I have noticed the demons they summon seem to belong in those environments. I do not know what use that information might have, but I told Lord Etherington regardless. He seemed pleased, but shooed me away before anyone could see us speaking.

Day 142

I am definitely losing weight. Is it vain to say I perhaps stare at myself longer in the mirror than I used to? My arms are leaner, my shoulders broader. My stomach is not flat, but it no longer bears a paunch. I have more energy, even if my mind feels befuddled with all the studying and training.

To say I am as lean and muscular as, say, Jamie Fitzroy (who is, according to an overheard conversation between Juno and a servant girl, the perfect male specimen) would be a lie.

But my confidence grows daily, and I earn grudging praise from Sir Caulder after each lesson. When we spar, Valentine and Tobias give up easily, for fear of being bruised by my wooden sword (as much as I would like to use my spatha, several experienced summoners are required for the barrier spell).

In any case, only Juno can stand against me—she is faster than me and I have earned lumps in our duels. Then again, I do not use my full strength against her—not because of any misplaced chivalry, but because I wish to surprise her in our mock tournament.

I wonder if she does the same. I am told she has taken to sparring with Jamie Fitzroy in her spare time. When the time comes to face her for real . . . I do not know what the outcome will be.

Day 145

I have not mentioned spellcraft in a while. In all honesty, that is because things are not going so well. You see, Mites have low mana. They recover it quickly, true, but it means that there are only so many spells I can practice before I run out.

Lucky for me, the shield spell can be reabsorbed into the body after being used, returning the majority of the mana to me. So, I am proficient in the shield spell, at least, even if my fireballs are a bit wonky and miss the makeshift target I have made in my room. It was hard enough having to explain the burn marks on the stone wall to the servants. Now, each time they change my bedding, they purse their lips with disapproval.

Day 157

I have made a discovery! I have been comparing Hominum's keys to all other symbols and languages that I can find. I have ruined my eyes in the countless hours I have spent examining ancient tomes in the library.

Finally, I have found something. Dwarven runes.

There are similarities there. Not identical matches to be sure, but one might guess that they follow the same root language.

Of course, even Lord Etherington scoffed at that. But I shall investigate further. I have discovered another treatise on the dwarves, which I have copied out in this diary.

TREATISE ON THE DWARVES
by Lord Edmund Raleigh

In recent years I have worked closely with several dwarves, perhaps more so than any other summoner, both common and noble. It has given me occasion to see their culture first-hand, and though I am no expert, I have been asked once again to write a treatise on one of the four races that inhabit our great continent.

When I announced my intentions to write this essay, it was met with some derision by my fellow nobles, who do not look so kindly upon the dwarves. This is in part due to the hostility that has historically existed between our peoples, which must be understood before dwarven society can be addressed.

Around two millennia ago, King Corwin led his people across the Akhad Desert to the east, arriving in what would one day come to be known as Hominum. These were the first humans to walk these lands but for a few traders and explorers. King Corwin's history is unknown, but it is said that he was banished from a great empire by his older brother, somewhere far to the west.

On arrival, King Corwin ingratiated himself with the native dwarves in their capital, a place that the humans called Corcillum. In exchange for sanctuary there, the humans built strong walls around the city to protect their new home from the orcs in the southern jungles. After a series of pitched battles, the humans were able to declare a truce on behalf of the dwarves.

For a time there was peace, until an albino orc declared war once more. The dwarves, who already had the habit of living belowground, used this to their advantage, protecting themselves from attack. Meanwhile, Corwin and his army retained a strong position behind their walls. The orc marauders turned their eyes to the elves instead, slaughtering them in a series of brutal raids across the northern territories. Once again, King Corwin and his army made a deal, this time with the elves.

Defeating the orcs at the Battle of Corcillum, Corwin and his nobles were taught the art of summoning in exchange for driving the orcs back into the jungles. Orc raids continue, however, and the culture of living belowground becomes ingrained in dwarven society.

A thousand years later, dwarves and humans live in relative harmony alongside one another. A council of dwarves rules in conjunction with the human king and his nobles. It is at this time that everything changed.

A great sickness brought by human traders from the west swept across the dwarven population, killing so many that soon humans outnumbered the dwarves. Where previously the balance of power had been relatively equal—the humans with their summoning ability, the dwarves with their greater numbers—now the humans had the advantage. Treacherously, the king slaughtered the council of dwarves at a meeting and began the process of subjugating their entire race.

It is here that our problems with the dwarves began, and continue to this day. Since then, it has been debated how many times the dwarves have attempted rebellions against the Hominum Empire. There have been four major insurrections, while several others might be considered riots that got out of hand. In general, dwarves believe they have rebelled and failed fourteen times. The main reasons for these uprisings are detailed below. A series of laws were enacted, the strictest being quotas in how many children dwarves could have. In doing so, dwarves were unable to recover their numbers and became a minority in their own land. To this day, the dwarven population has never exceeded more than a few thousand.

Other laws were put in place to limit dwarven prosperity and power. It was made illegal for dwarves to own land, and they were forced into a small ghetto in the center of Corcillum, where they could be watched and kept together. I have visited this place on many occasions, and though the surrounding buildings are decrepit, the dwarves have made a garden of their home, making up for their lack of space by digging deeper.

The last dwarven insurrection was around two hundred years ago, but even today, rumors of potential troubles abound. Dwarves are still considered untrustworthy by most humans, and racial violence and hatred continue. That being said, there are some humans who sympathize with the dwarves, and it is not unheard of for half-human, half-dwarven children to be born in illicit trysts between lovers of different races. Unfortunately, it is said that these children suffer terribly, rejected by both sides. Most make their way across the Vesanian Sea to the west, where such prejudice does not exist.

Throughout his reign, King Alfric has expanded and ruthlessly enforced the old laws and enacted further limitations on his dwarven subjects. They may not join the military, for fear that they will learn the art of warfare. Curfews prevent dwarves from walking the streets at night, and dwarves are not allowed to gather in groups larger than three, so they are forced to travel underground when visiting one another in the evenings.

Weapons are not allowed to be worn by dwarves in public—something that all adult dwarves, both male and female, have a religious and traditional obligation to do. This has led to many dwarven arrests, and their prison population is significantly higher than that of others. Alfric is also in control of our police force, the Pinkertons, who are instructed to be suspicious of dwarves. I suspect the dwarves are given far worse treatment than humans when stopped. It is not unknown for dwarves to return home from work with broken bones, or worse, after a run-in with the Pinkertons.

Dwarven goods are now taxed at a significantly higher rate than that of humans, making their wares more expensive to produce. However, dwarves have remained competitive by being extremely skilled and specialized artisans, far surpassing their human counterparts. In particular, they excel in ceramics, textiles, mechanisms and of course, weaponry. These weapons are particularly coveted because they are often made from dwarven steel, far sharper and stronger than normal metals, but notoriously difficult to work with. The secret to creating this alloy is one of the dwarves' most closely guarded.

Dwarves produce their merchandise within their own homes to protect their secrets. As such, dwarven homes are designed to contain workshops and other such studios deep underground. It is not unusual for one of these structures to contain a central chimney, running from the basement to the large, plush tent that remains permanently erected above their underground homes. This chimney keeps the home warm and allows dwarves to do activities such as pottery and blacksmithing. In fact, some dwarven homes have the space to contain their very own baths and saunas.

Dwarves have also learned that by spiraling the stairway in their underground homes counterclockwise, an attacker's sword arm would be encumbered by the pillar in its center when fighting downward. This makes dwarven homes incredibly difficult to invade. They also have strong metal doors that protect different sections of the home, meaning they need not fight at all if they wish not to. Networks of tunnels between homes allow for escape, but also allow warriors to reinforce one another should they need assistance, and spring up to attack an enemy from behind should such a strategy be required.

Dwarven religion is taken very seriously by most dwarves. The females wear veils to protect their modesty and to ensure that the men marry them for their personalities rather than out of attraction. When they mature, dwarven women are given a sharpened or spiked bracelet known as a torque. Since this is not considered a weapon by the Pinkertons, it is far rarer that female dwarves are arrested.

In contrast, dwarven men do not shave or cut their hair. This stems from their belief that if the creator wanted them to have shorter hair, he would have given them shorter hair. They choose to remain in his image. Their hair is often braided and oiled to remain clean and out of the way, and some even wear turbans to keep it in place.

At maturity dwarven males are given a small axe, which they are to carry with them at all times. It is also common to see dwarven men with tattoos, though this is more of a cultural than religious requirement.

Dwarves are small in stature, with the very tallest reaching an adult human's sternum, while a shorter dwarf might reach man's navel. However, a dwarf's strength is unmatched, as they are barrel-chested and muscular. Despite not being allowed military training, they have a reputation for being dangerous fighters.

Boars are popular pets among dwarves, used in much the same way as we do horses and mules. Historically, dwarves rode chariots into battle, but these days boars are used to draw carts loaded with goods. That being said, the boars are formidable creatures, with dangerous tusks and a powerful charge.

Finally, I must address dwarven foods and drinks. I must confess to having a particular fondness for their cooking, as well as their excellent beer. Many a night I have passed in the Anvil Tavern (an excellent dwarven establishment) on my way to the north. Dwarven beer is a secret recipe, so I am forced to buy several casks whenever I pass through. It is worth the expense.

As for dwarven food, their fried root vegetables and meat dumplings are to die for. And with that, I must close this treatise. The tavern awaits!

Day 178

The days go by slowly now. I practice the same battle spells over and over. It feels I shall not improve much more. So, I have sought out other spells. The nobles seem to practice only the same four as we commoners do. Perhaps . . . I can find a way of beating them by mastering one that nobody else is using.

Back to the books.

Day 189

With a little help from Lady Sinclair, I have begun to compile a list of spells that may prove useful in the future. You can find them written in this volume. Of course, there are thousands of spells. But many of them are variations of the same thing, others too complicated and high in mana-cost. You would not believe the size of one book I found, dedicated purely to changing the colors of wyrdlights. Hundreds of spells!

In any case, I have slowly begun to practice some of the spells. They are hard—far harder than the battle spells. But I suppose that's why they are not used. No matter. I shall persevere.

Day 198

The frost spell and the cat's-eye spell are all I have been able to pull off so far. Interestingly, the former is a recent discovery by Electra (found inside a Polarion) and has not made it into Hominum's official curriculum. I barely have enough mana to pull off even a single instance of the others. I do dearly love Sable, but I wonder how much better off I would be with a demon that has more mana.

I mustn't think such things though. She can sense my disappointment.

Day 204

I begged Lord Cavendish to help me capture a new demon today. Since we began our summoning lessons, we have been focused on demonic control. We also watch him send his demon into the ether—once he even sent his second demon, a Lutra, to swim in a small brook that flowed through the ether's jungles.

We have also practiced powering up pentacles and creating minuscule portals of our own, barely larger than a fist (but large enough for Sable to pass through, I have noticed). Unfortunately, I cannot hold one open long enough to send Sable safely through—it fizzles, shrinks and disappears on occasion. If Sable was on the other side when that happened, unable to get through, I would lose her forever.

Even if I was able to hold the portal open steadily, my mana would run out quickly—I would barely have any time at all to capture another Mite!

So I asked Lord Cavendish to hold one open for me—to let me hunt. I could capture a lesser Mite, I think. Have Sable drag it through the portal, hold it over the pentacle and allow me to infuse it, thus capturing the creature.

They are weak, base demons, but it would give me more mana, and another set of eyes, another distraction.

But Lord Cavendish refused, saying it would be better to wait until second year, when I was more experienced. He asked me what my rush was, and I had no answer for him.

So, it will be just Sable and I going into battle.

Day 219

The days blur into one now. It's quite depressing, sitting down and looking at you, dear journal, and finding I have nothing new to report.

I eat alone, I study alone. Lord Etherington is right. I could not stand another year like this. Am I truly so unlikable? No matter how hard I try with the other commoners, they avoid me like the plague. Perhaps it is easier for them, to have a scapegoat, an enemy. The nobles and teachers are just as hard on them as they are on me. It can't be easy for them either.

Day 220

We have been given a date for the mock tournament! So as not to clash with the real tournament that the second-years shall be taking part in, it will take place in a month's time. I am glad of it.

There is a flattening of the learning curve when it comes to spell-craft and demonic control, not to mention swordcraft. I am ahead of the others, but my rate of improvement has slowed and they are beginning to catch up. Even my body has slowed in its changes—I cannot shift a layer of puppy fat from my stomach and arms.

Sir Caulder has told me not to worry—it will lend weight to my swings and put the others in a false sense of security. I can't tell if he's trying to make me feel better.

Maybe only one rasher of bacon tomorrow.

Day 221

Who am I kidding? This bacon is too damned good. I had four, and two eggs and some toast with jam besides. Whoops.

In other news, our exams are next week. In all honesty I have barely noticed their approach. I have been studying flat-out since I came here, and I am far ahead of everyone else. I should pass with fly-ing colors.

Day 227

I went back to Electra with my findings on the orc runes. I had not been back to her since our first encounter—Lord Etherington had banned me from doing so for fear of drawing attention. But I couldn't hold back.

In any case, she was not as dismissive as Lord Etherington was. She has asked Jeffrey to investigate—sending him to the Anvil Tavern to see if he can learn more about the dwarfish language. He seemed disgusted by the proposal when she called him to the room. I don't think anything will come of it.

Day 228

Exams. I trounced them. I walked out of the lecture hall a full hour before anyone else.

Day 229

Damn. Did I spell "Catoblepas" correctly on that last question? I can't remember.

I'm sure I got its classifications, summoning level and everything else correct. Surely they can't take marks off for that?

Day 230

Lord Etherington is a sneaky man. Today we were told that in between rounds of our mock tournament, our mana could be recharged using a charging stone. That's a small cylinder made up of corundum crystals of the same color—it can be filled up with mana by a summoner to be used later. Apparently it is used on our front lines quite often to sustain shield spells throughout the night when orc shamans rain fireballs down on our trenches.

Anyway, providing a charging stone was a way to give us commoners a better chance at winning, since we would likely use up all our mana in the first round (given we only have a single level-one Mite each and so little mana to begin with). We could refill our "jar" of mana (if I remember correctly the metaphor Lord Cavendish used) between rounds.

Then again, the nobles would be fully charged again too. Even now, I'm not quite sure if it will be an advantage. But the way Lord Etherington sees it, it is better to face a more powerful opponent with some mana of your own than a weaker opponent with no mana. In the latter situation, I would be helpless.

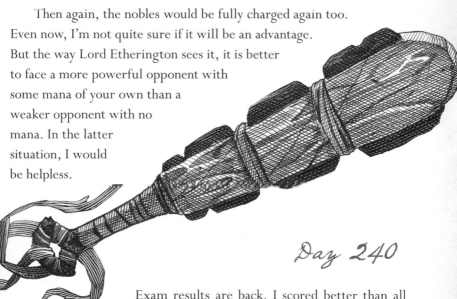

Day 240

Exam results are back. I scored better than all the others, even the golden boy, Jamie Fitzroy, but it seems none of the teachers care. Not even Lord Etherington. Perhaps they used to be important, but now that there is a war on, the entire curriculum seems to be weighted toward the tournaments.

No matter. I shall excel there also.

Day 250

It is today. Our mock tournament. I found I could barely sleep last night. Nor could I practice my spells, or exercise. I needed to be fully charged and rested for the tournament.

For once, I did not eat any bacon at all for breakfast. My stomach was in knots. Almost a year of training, and it all came down to this. I could slip on the sand and be out in the first round.

Then what? Another year of solitude and probable inadequacy, followed by eventual death on the front lines.

Still, my success in the exams gives me heart. One form of practice had paid off. Perhaps my other training will see me through this.

Now I must leave my room and go down to the atrium. It is about to begin.

Day 251

This is what happened.

We were walked down the long line of jail cells, a stark reminder that the leaders of Vocans had thought the war so terrifying that they would need these for deserters. Here we were battling for the right to fight in it, and perhaps earn a safer posting.

Of course, now they just shot deserters on the spot. Much simpler.

When we reached the sands of the arena, I was surprised at the number of people in the audience. It seemed most of the servants had shown up to watch, as had the teachers, Provost Scipio and even a few parents—though clearly only the nobles' parents had been allowed to attend. I wonder what my own parents would have thought, had they seen me here. It didn't bear thinking about.

Strangest of all was the general. There was only one, a jolly-looking man whose nose was beet red from drink, his uniform garishly covered

in medals and tassels. He swigged from a hip flask as we looked at him. Clearly this was more of a jaunt away from the front lines than serious consideration, but the other commoners perked up at the sight of him. As far as they were concerned, he was the man to impress.

When I glanced at the nobles, I saw they seemed barely bothered by the onlookers. I wasn't surprised. Most of them would end up taking commissions in their parents' battalions, however they performed. This was more a chance to show off for them, if anything.

"We have separated the tournament into two brackets, to keep things fair: the commoners in one and the nobles in the other. The winners of each bracket will fight each other for the victory," Provost Scipio announced.

This made sense—it was a win for everyone. We commoners would be guaranteed to get to at least second place, while it spared most of the nobles the risk of embarrassment of being beaten by one of us.

He announced the bracket contenders, but all I remember now was that my first round would be against Valentine. We were given no details about what each round would entail; instead, we were led back down the corridor of cells and locked in.

It seemed a while before the first round started—and servants wheeling cloth-covered handcarts hurried back and forth, though for what purpose it was impossible to tell. Finally, Sir Caulder came for the first two combatants—two nobles.

Then all I could do was wait and listen to the cheers of the crowd as the nobles went at it. I strained to hear the sound of spells, but the noise was hard to distinguish.

So instead, I stroked Sable's carapace, soothing both her and myself as her feelings of well-being traveled down the umbilical cord of our consciousnesses.

I don't know how many rounds took place before it was my turn. I only remember Sir Caulder rapping on the bars of my cell with my spatha. I reached out for it as he unlocked me, but he kept it out of reach.

"Not this round," was all he said.

I trudged into the arena and was shocked to find they had dramatically changed its interior while I had been inside the cells. What had once been a sandy pit was now filled with water. Carriage wheel–sized islands of sand had been piled haphazardly around it, but in most places it seemed knee deep. In the very center, there was a much larger island, perhaps as large as four carriages placed alongside one another.

Across from me, I could see Valentine perched on a wooden platform built on the rim of the arena opposite me, and Sir Caulder gently led me to my own. From my new vantage, I could see the entire arena, but clearly I myself was not supposed to enter.

"The rules are very simple," Provost Scipio called from the crowd. "You may not leave the platforms or you will be disqualified. Your demons must battle each other in the arena. They may not kill—it will result in disqualification. Only kinetic and shield spells may be used.

The winner will have complete dominance of the central island for thirty seconds. Begin!"

I barely had time to register his words before Valentine's Mite, Amon, was zooming toward the island in the arena's center. Then Sable shot from her perch on my shoulder.

Valentine had a scrying crystal in his hand—a mistake, in my humble opinion, though at the time I worried I should have done the same with Sable. But it was too late now; the demons clashed in midair, and I could feel the pain of it pulse down my consciousness.

From my platform, I could see the two demons perfectly, battling back and forth across the island, no longer in the air but tumbling in each other's grips on the sand below. While Valentine's mind would have been filled with the dual sounds coming from both his own ears and Amon's, I had no such distraction. He kept glancing at the stone, but I imagine all he could see was flashes of mandibles and sand.

There was little I could do to direct Sable, and I cursed my lack of preparation. I had been so focused on myself that Sable's training had been limited to demonic control. Here, that now seemed virtually useless.

For agonizing minutes, the two Mites fought along the sand, occasionally parting and staring at each other, before launching themselves into the fray once more.

As the battle went on, I wondered at how it could possibly end— the demons seemed well matched and neither would cede the island. In fact, even if this was the very last of the first-bracket rounds, it must have been going on for far longer than the others would have taken.

I found myself glancing at the crowd. Their cheering had abruptly silenced after the first few minutes, reduced to a low muttering. Was this boring for them? Even the general seemed to be sleeping, his chin resting on his chest.

But no. Many of the onlookers had smiles on their faces, bemused. In fact, Provost Scipio was positively laughing. What was so funny? Even as I considered this, I caught Lord Etherington's eye. The man was sitting near the back, and his eyes flashed with meaning I could not perceive. He couldn't risk showing me favor.

Then I saw his finger, gesticulating wildly in his lap. He was pointing at Valentine, or so it seemed. What was I missing?

It hit me. We weren't allowed to leave our platforms. But that didn't mean we couldn't use spells against each other! Provost Scipio had purposefully worded the rules to confuse us.

As Valentine stared at his scrying crystal, I etched the telekinesis symbol behind my back and gathered a ball of shimmering kinetic energy. Knowing that I could replenish my reserves and that this would be my best chance to win, I put my all into it.

Then, even as Valentine looked up as the crowd noticed what I was doing and cheered, I released the ball with careful aim.

With only a Mite's mana to use, the ball was not big. But when it connected with him, taking him in his midriff, it was enough to send him head over heels into the crowd behind him, landing sprawled along the general's lap, who was given a rude awakening.

"James wins!" Scipio announced, roaring with laughter.

I did not know who was more red-faced, Valentine or the general.

. . .

Another long wait, followed by a quick stop to the charging stone where I felt the mana run like ice back into my body. Then Sir Caulder was marching me down the corridor once more. For some reason I imagined that it would be different, but it remained the same water-logged arena. This time though, the wooden platforms had been obliterated. It would seem that two nobles had fought in the round following mine—no commoner would have been capable of doing such damage.

In any case, I saw my opponent across from me. Juno, staring at me with a focus that bordered on fury. Her chosen weapon, a cutlass, was held unwaveringly in her hand, and I could immediately see from her stance that she had been holding back in her sparring sessions too.

Her stance was different from the one we had been taught by Sir Caulder; it was the kind the nobles used in the few times we had seen them practicing. Of course, I had known that she was taking private lessons with Jamie Fitzroy, but I had thought it was more of an excuse so they could canoodle together.

Yet here she was in what Sir Caulder had told me was a fencing stance. One designed purely for success against other swordsmen, but relatively useless when doing battle with an orc.

I could see our teachers and three other summoners standing together beside the arena, their fingers etching a complex glyph in the air. As I gripped my sword, I could feel a strange slipperiness between my fingers, and it was then I realized that the barrier spell sheathed me: a near-invisible protection from cuts and spells.

"Swordplay only!" Provost Scipio announced. "No spells, no demons. The summoner who is determined to have struck a killing blow first shall be the winner of this round. Begin!"

I took a moment to direct Sable to sit on the edge of the arena and not to interfere. That was my mistake. While my mind sent intentions to my demon, Juno was sloshing across the arena. Before I had jumped down into the water myself, Juno had taken a stand in the large island in the center.

Now I faced an uphill battle, and while my feet would be slowed by water, hers would be unencumbered. I shivered at the coldness of the water, then I circled her, keeping ten feet of distance between us, but she followed my movements, skirting the edge of the island, her sword held aloft.

There was a smaller island near one side of her own, barely large enough for me to stand on. I took my place there and waited too. Now, it was a game of patience. One of us would have to attack the other from a position of weakness.

"Battle must end in twenty minutes, or you shall both be disqualified," Scipio announced from the seats, seeing what was about to happen.

I shrugged, suggesting my indifference, but Juno grinned in response. She knew how much training I had done. Knew that I wanted to use my spatha, at least once. I wouldn't let the timer tick down and lose that way.

Still, my island was so close to hers that she could not let her guard down. Each time her cutlass began to drop to her side, I faked a move toward her and she was forced to bring her guard up once more.

I could see the sweat trickle from her brow. She might have trained in techniques from high-paid fencing masters alongside her beau, but she hadn't put in the physical training that I had. Her arms would be leaden by now.

But . . . already ten minutes or so had passed, and she wasn't budging. So, I did the only thing left to me. I charged.

As I splashed through the water toward her, I lashed out with a foot, sending a gout of water at her face. She barely blinked, but it was enough to give me time to sweep my sword from on high, cutting toward her shoulder. Our blades met with a clash, and my blade swept down her own until we were face-to-face, straining against each other. Already I could feel myself gaining the upper hand, for with our blades crossed at the hilts, there she could not maneuver her sword.

Now it was a contest of strength and stamina. She leaned her head back, then thrust forward with fierce abandon. I saw stars as her forehead struck the bridge of my nose, but I persevered. Her knee snaked between my legs, but I dodged aside. Then, she collapsed back and I was able to sweep my spatha down and touch my blade to her throat.

"James wins!" I heard Scipio bellow, and I held out a hand to help her up. She ignored it and stalked away.

Then it was over.

. . .

The final round. This time there was almost no wait at all. Barely time to recharge my mana before I was being marched back to the arena.

My heart sank as I saw the opponent waiting there, though I shouldn't have been surprised. Jamie Fitzroy, staring daggers at me across the waterlogged desert. I had defeated his beau. It was personal for him.

"The rules here are simple," Provost Scipio called out, and I could feel the slipperiness of the barrier spell once more.

"Spells may be used. Demons may only attack each other, and neither they nor their summoners may permanently injure or kill, only incapacitate. The first to strike a killing blow, or the first to incapacitate the other's demon, wins."

I could see Jamie's demon and thanked the heavens that it could not fly too. I had no plan of engaging it, for it was far more powerful than my own. It was a Felid—a common-enough demon among nobles by all accounts but no less deadly. It bore a leonine mane, giving it a fierce appearance, but if I flew Sable up far enough, the demon element would be neutralized. There was no way a Mite could defeat a Felid.

"Begin!" Scipio yelled, and together we jumped into the arena.

Immediately I threw up a shield, and just in time too. No sooner had I etched the spell and the oval of opaque material had appeared than a ball of flame erupted on its outside, knocking me back a foot. Sable was safely on my shoulder, but I could see Jamie's Felid was haring across the water toward me, sharing none of a typical feline's distaste for water.

I reinforced my shield, leaving just enough mana within me for a single fireball of my own. Jamie likely had another twenty fireballs within him at least, but he was being cautious too—he had a shield of his own.

Now the Felid was a few feet away, so I sent Sable flying high into the air. Immediately, Jamie released a ball of kinetic energy that smashed into the ceiling above the crowd. There was a gasp, for it had come close to striking them.

"Parents, if you would be so kind," Scipio barked.

Light shone around me, and then I saw an opaque shield forming around the arena. The crowd as now safe from high-flying spells.

The Felid drew to a stop, snarling at me but coming no closer. As for Sable, she flew with all her might in a zigzag pattern near the ceiling, while below, Jamie pointed his finger at her, squinting down it like the barrel of a gun.

I had no choice but to advance upon him—Sable could only avoid his spells for so long. Soon I was within a dozen feet, and as I etched a fireball symbol of my own, his eyes turned back to me, but not before sending one last shimmering ball of kinetic energy at Sable. I felt a stab of pain as she was blown aside by the impact on the ceiling, but she remained aloft.

"Come closer, common muck," Jamie snarled, and I was shocked at his anger then. Not to mention the hypocrisy, given he was upset over me beating his commoner girlfriend. We were both standing in the water now—Jamie had chosen a spot with no land nearby.

We squared up to each other, and I drew my spatha, letting the fireball symbol fizzle and die. If I got close enough, I might just be able to use my blade faster than he could etch an attack spell.

He advanced, until our shields pressed against each other, and then slowly he heaved forward, pushing me back. I could have held him if I wanted to, maybe even pushed him back, but there was an island behind me and I let him push me there, wading back through the water. Then I braced myself against the sand and grinned at the look of surprise on his face as his show of strength was halted.

I had the high ground now, and he would be slow to move his feet in the water. But with the large shields between us, I could not hope to use my spatha, even if I dove to one side of it.

No, I would have to think of something else. I ran through my options, while Jamie took the opportunity to fire a blast of kinetic energy toward the ceiling, not aiming it but letting it out in a wave of power. I felt Sable slam against the ceiling, but she stoically held on, refusing to be knocked from the air.

In that moment, I noticed something. Jamie's shield only extended as far as his knees—it did not go beneath the water as mine did. A fireball would not go through water, and a kinetic blast would lose its energy as it pushed through. But lightning—it would be doubly effective in the water . . . and I was standing on land.

In truth I was shocked, if you'll pardon the pun, that nobody had thought of it earlier, but then in the last two rounds, using lightning spells had not been an option.

Jamie's eyes widened as I hurriedly etched the lightning symbol, but as he surged toward the land I fired everything I had into the water. The surface crackled, and blue lightning sizzled about his body, but of course the barrier spell protected him.

I unleashed a triumphant shout, waiting for Provost Scipio to announce my victory. But there was nothing, only the sound of Jamie panting as he maneuvered himself onto the small island beside me.

"I won!" I yelled over my shoulder.

"I reached the land in time," Jamie yelled back.

"Liar," I snarled, but Scipio's silence told me who he believed. Now I was left with no mana but for that stored in my shield.

"Face it," Jamie snarled, "you're done."

But I wasn't done.

Now was the time to consider my other spells, and I cursed myself for not thinking of it sooner. Frost . . . that also worked better in water, but it was a mana-heavy spell, and it took time to etch. I would need to absorb my shield to be able to afford it, and for that I needed a distraction.

"Sable, now!" I yelled.

Jamie's eyes shot up, and in that moment I shoved hard with my shield, sending him tumbling back into the water. As Jamie sputtered, holding his shield in front of him in case of an attack from sword or spell, I absorbed the opaque barrier.

I blasted ice around him, encasing his lower body in a solid block. Jamie's finger swirled.

Then nothing.

• • •

So here I am, a day later. Sitting in the infirmary, my belongings laid out beside me. Jamie won, of course. I may have trapped him in ice, but the barrier kept his body from pain and damage. So he blasted me with kinetic energy, slamming me into the arena wall so hard that I fell unconscious.

It gives me heart that the servants had to haul him out and hack the ice from his legs. And I believe, no matter what the others think of me, they'll know I am no pushover. I could have played it better—the water was something I should have used sooner. But surely I did well enough for Lord Etherington to commission me early.

Sable is alive and well, snoozing on my shoulder as I write this. I too am exhausted. Nobody came to see me today but Dame Fairhaven, who had no information other than what I just told you. Not even Lord Etherington.

So I'm going to bed. Perhaps he will come tomorrow.

Day 252

A carriage was waiting for me. It was Lord Cavendish who told me, and he had a sorrowful look upon his face when he did so. He did not need to come all the way up the tower, where the infirmary was, to inform me. He could have passed the message to a servant; instead he came himself.

But if he had wanted to lecture me, he must not have found the words, for he stood dumbly as I packed my things. It was only when I had said good-bye and was halfway down the stairs that he called after me.

"He's not your friend, James!"

Too late to back out now. I was sad to be leaving Vocans, strange though that was. Despite my loneliness, I had found joy in the discovery of new knowledge, and finding that inner strength I did not know I had. And Sir Caulder, Dame Fairhaven, even Lord Cavendish, had all treated me well enough. I shall miss them, I think.

So now the carriage rumbles down south, toward the front lines. It seems Lord Etherington kept his promise. There was a new uniform waiting for me in the carriage, and I wear it as I write this. An officer's uniform. I am a second lieutenant.

• • •

The carriage driver led me to my quarters, a tent identical to a hundred others drawn up along the edge of the trenches. Then he left me, hurrying back to his carriage in the hopes of returning to Corcillum before it gets too late. Already the sun is setting—our journey was a long one, and we left in the late afternoon.

This is a strange place. The ground has been churned raw by the tramp of thousands of feet, and campfires extend to the east and west as far as the eye can see. This is where civilization ends and the wilds begin.

Men play music on harmonicas or violins, and drinking seems to be rife here. Soldiers sleep where they fall in drunken stupors, while others laugh, sing and fight.

There is no note for me inside my tent, where the ground is no more than trodden straw and my bed is a wooden bunk. The only other furniture is a rotting trunk and a rickety desk and chair.

Some thoughtful soul has left me a hand mirror, but it is more likely so I can shave and look presentable, as an officer should. How were they to know I have barely begun to whisker?

I clutch Sable to my chest, warming her beneath my shirt, and try not to let my thoughts drift to home. In truth, I have given my mother

and father as little thought as possible over the past few months. It is too painful.

They had thought I would be safe at Vocans, rubbing shoulders with the elite, setting myself up for a grand career. Instead, I am in a muddy field, a stone's throw away from the end of civilization.

As I toss and turn on my bunk, I wonder if this place will be better than Vocans. It is a man's world here. The thought that I might be expected to lead such men as those outside fills me with terror. I can only imagine their reaction to my boyish voice ordering them into danger.

So I wait . . . or hide.

The sounds of revelry outside haunt me. It shall be a long night.

Day 253

Lord Etherington is here! It seems in hiring me, he has abandoned his position as demonology teacher at the academy. I received a summons from a grizzled sergeant, who ducked into my tent without a word and handed me my orders. I have fixed the note here, for posterity.

Lieutenant Baker,

You are to report to the mustering ground of the Eighth Battalion at 1300 hours.

Commander Etherington

The sergeant took pity on me, his eyes widening in surprise as he took in my age. He offered to lead me to the mustering ground.

Outside, the ground was muddy from a light drizzle from the night before, but there was a semblance of order now. Men marching back and forth, others lined up within the dark trench that lay directly in front of my tent, scattered with small stone and wood forts, their tops bristling with cannons.

The trench was so deep as to have to step on a wooden stair built along its inside to see over the top. There, men stared out into a no - man's-land, cleared out by fire. The ground was cratered and torn between it and the green of the jungle, ravaged by the explosions of shaman spells and the furrowing of cannonballs.

I could see red uniforms strewn along the jungle edge. Corpses, too close to the enemy territory to warrant collecting. I forced myself to look, to take it all in. This was my new existence.

The mustering ground was little more than a parcel of land squared off beside the tents by four long ropes. There, around three hundred men stood at attention, muskets with bayonets affixed held tight and upright against their shoulders.

The officers were scattered among them, but fortunately the sergeant who had come to collect me motioned to a likely spot at the head of the parade to the far right. It seemed to me that the soldiers there were almost as young as I was. Younger in fact than the rest of the column, as if they had been selected specifically. Were these to be the men I commanded? It seemed so, for they eyed me with trepidation when I walked there.

No sooner had I found my place than Lord Etherington emerged from his tent—one far larger than my own and filled with plush furs, if the glimpse I had of the interior was anything to go by.

For some reason I had thought he would introduce me. But instead, he simply walked back and forth, stopping here and there to talk to the officers and inspect his men more closely.

Finally, he dismissed us, and the sergeants bellowed orders as the men were sent to their duties. It seemed that most of what they did was related to rationing of food and firewood, maintaining of uniforms and filling in and digging new latrines. My own men were given the latter job, and the groans were clearly audible as the sergeant—who I now realized was the sergeant of my platoon—sent them scurrying in the direction of a foul stench somewhere to the north.

I regretted acting so green around him, but he seemed kind enough. Then Lord Etherington approached me and we were alone together in the emptying mustering ground.

"Settling in okay?" he asked, giving me a quick smile.

"Well enough," I replied.

"Your first mission is tomorrow. We've been moving deeper into orc territory over the past few years, burning our way forward and digging new trenches. This used to be all jungle. There was an orc village here, a ways over there. Of course the soldiers tore most of it down before I got wind of it, and the flames burned the rest, but there's a hut there that's still intact. You're to go investigate it."

"Why haven't you done it?"

He glared at me then.

"What did I bring you here for? Can't you get into your thick skull that I cannot show interest in studying those savages?"

Of course. I bowed my head as he strode off.

I looked around, but my men had gone, and there was nothing else to do. So here I am in my tent, dragging this entry out as long as possible.

Tomorrow, my research begins.

Day 254

After muster this morning, my men were once again dispatched to latrine duty. The hut was derelict, and I could see the charred remains of those that had once surrounded it nearby. I was surprised it was still standing, and that the ribald soldiers some few hundred yards away had not destroyed it for firewood. It seemed that only one thing had kept them from doing so, that was obvious.

It was the symbols daubed on the walls outside it. Superstition had kept the soldiers at bay, fear of some form of curse or trap. I had no such qualms, recognizing the symbols as the four primary battle spells, and ducked through the straw awning that still covered the entrance.

The inside was made of primitive wooden boards, with a thatched roof that was falling through, allowing me some light as I examined the inside. The floor was made of flattened bamboo, and there was no furniture to speak of. There was not much to be seen.

At first glance, that is.

The walls. Someone, and I mean *someone* rather than something, had painted on the walls. An ocean, of startling detail. Above, I could see Ropen flying, strange, featherless bird demons with stretched membrane wings and elongated headrests. Of particular interest was that each one had a symbol written above it . . . a number. Orcs did not use numbers often, so theirs were a series of lines, crossed out when they reached five—rather like what prisoners scratched on the interiors of

their cells. The symbol represented the number four; the Ropen's summoning level.

Then I saw it. Another creature, lying on an island painted on the wall. I did not recognize it, which meant this was a new demon entirely! Never heard of or seen before in all of Hominum's history.

Above it was the symbol for fifteen and farther still, orcish letters. In my studies at Vocans, I had been able to determine the pronunciation of orcish words, even if the language was still alien to me. These I had paid particular attention to, for if I was to learn anything from the orcs in my studies, I would need to learn their language.

Here, it pronounced a two-syllable word: Akhlut. As for the demon itself, it was similar to the orca: a killer whale. I had never seen one in person, but the sailors who frequented the tavern had spoken of them in great detail.

With the same white markings along its belly and around its eyes, and the enormous fluke tail behind it, the key difference was the four clawed legs curled beneath it. A land whale, and a ferocious one at that. No wonder it was level fifteen.

Already I had learned something new, added to Hominum's knowledge. It wasn't a game changer by any means but . . . it was something. Proof perhaps that we *could* learn from the orcs.

Alas, there was nothing more of use in the hut, except for what looked like the tattered remnants of a summoning leather, no different from our own but for the fur that still clung to one side of it.

I stayed a while longer, more out of a desire to avoid another lonely day in my tent than from the belief that something else could be there. I even tried digging around in the ground with my spatha, but found nothing.

So now I have returned, as the sun sets, and another night of raucous revelry begins outside.

Day 260

Lord Etherington is pleased. He wrote to Provost Scipio and told him of my discovery. Apparently Dame Fairhaven has added it to the official demonology on the Vocans curriculum, though apparently it annoyed the new teacher, somebody named Major Goodwin. The best part is, even Lord Etherington could not take credit for my discovery—he is too high and mighty to insinuate that he himself has been investigating orc ruins. I have to admit, it makes me feel like it's all worthwhile . . . at least today.

Day 267

The days here are hard. It has been two weeks since Lord Etherington gave me something to investigate. So, I have been told to take control of my soldiers.

There is not much to do. They resent me, and I do not blame them. Lord Etherington thought he did me a kindness by putting together a platoon of youngsters. But because they are young, they are given the worst jobs. Latrine duty mostly, or digging trenches, collecting firewood. The other officers had agreed this the very first morning, and I am too fearful to object. These are full-fledged noble battlemages. How can I, a teenage commoner, stand up to them?

I eat alone in the officers' mess and feel lonelier than ever. To think, at least at Vocans the teachers would talk to me. Here, it is only Lord Etherington, and forced, polite conversations with my sergeant.

Each morning I assign my soldiers their tasks, as if I had chosen them myself (when in truth, the task is handed to me by the captain). They glare at me and move on.

I have begged Lord Etherington to be transferred to a different platoon, but he scoffs at me and tells me to grow a pair. I don't know what he means by that.

Day 285

Electra has been sending me letters. It is a blessed relief to have someone to talk to, albeit via the medium of scrawled parchment. Sable delivers my letters to her overnight, flying my roll of parchment up to her tower and returning with her reply.

She has been instructing me in the art of dissection. I have glued some of her diagrams of dissected demons to this page—the scraps of parchment are small, so that Sable can bear their weight.

I cram as much writing as I can onto each of my replies, but it seems there is never enough space.

Day 301

The front lines have moved forward. The entire army fired a volley into the jungle, the sound like a thunderclap in the sky, the stench like rotten eggs as the sulphurous white smoke wafted behind the soldiers.

Then they charged toward the jungle, leaping over the ramparts and taking up positions along the jungle edge. My lads were sent to start digging right away, along with a few other platoons. Meanwhile, the jungle was set aflame and more volleys were poured into its dark interior, for fear of orcs lurking within.

As the work continued into the night, the entire forest seemed to become a hellscape as the red inferno stretched up into the sky. I leaped into the trenches with my men, and together we dug in the scorching heat that blew in from the jungle, sweating and swearing until we were coated in black mud and stared at one another through smoke-reddened eyes.

Eventually the flames slowly burned themselves out, until the light drizzle finished them off. As we trudged our way back to the makeshift washrooms back at the camp,

which was already being dismantled and moved up to our new front lines, the men looked at me with grudging respect. A noble officer would never lift a finger to do the men's work, let alone sully their uniform digging trenches in the rain, heat and mud.

As I walk by, another officer catches the chevrons on my shoulder and glares at me. I shrug and continue on. Fraternizing with the soldiers is not encouraged, nor is such unseemly behavior as what he had just witnessed. But the other officers already look down on me, and that will never change. As for my men . . . we shall see.

Tomorrow, I shall join my men in latrine duty, and every other task from here on in.

Day 302

Clearing out the latrines is the worst. That is all.

Day 310

Sergeant Daniels, my sergeant, approves of what I am doing, though he is a little annoyed. Since I am mucking in with the men, it would be unseemly for him to stand to the side, so he has to join in too.

And I have met another common summoner! His name is Arcturus. It's strange that he only has one name. He introduced himself as Arcturus, but is also called Captain Arcturus by the other officers, as if it is his second name. Curious. We spoke only briefly, but he introduced me to a few other commoners, who I now sit with in the officers' mess hall during mealtimes. I had not even thought to check if there were other commoners here—I assumed everyone was noble, for some strange reason. Almost all the commoners are second or first lieutenants, and one is even Arcturus's brother. They are nice enough, but apparently rumors of my studying of the orcs have spread among the officers. The nobles think me a fool, while the commoners think me one whose unpopularity might rub off on them.

Still, these few don't seem to mind too much. Oh! It sure does feel good to have someone to talk to.

Day 320

There has been a battle. Not near my part of the front lines, thank heavens, but somewhere far down to the west, near Raleighshire. It happened just an hour ago, in the dead of night. The orcs charged the trenches and slaughtered half the men before the Celestial Corps arrived and fought them off.

It is unclear how they reached the trenches without being mowed down by gunfire and shrapnel from the cannons. But that's beside the point; there are battles every other night somewhere or other. The real reason I am telling you this is because there were shamans involved in this battle. Which means fresh demon corpses!

Electra has her hands full studying plants—she has found an enterprising young summoner to bring them to her from the ether, and apparently the servant Jeffrey has been helping her. She thinks he might even become her apprentice someday.

I must admit, I'm a little jealous.

Anyway, the dead demons are being sent over. I shall begin my dissection tomorrow.

Day 321

It stank to high heavens, most likely for being left in the warm morning air too long. Lacking any work space or tools, I was forced to use my work desk and spatha in their stead. I needed privacy, as there were a dozen men standing outside, staring at the strange creature left for me in a wheelbarrow outside.

So I performed the dissection within my tent. I really, really hope the smell will go away. As I write this, I have my nose plugged up with rags. The stench is quite potent.

The demon was an Enenra—a shadow demon. Few summoners have ever captured one, and entries in the library about them were scant, if I recall. I must have read every book there, so it was pointless traveling back to research it anymore.

Apparently, when seen in the wild, it appears as a smoky shadow, flowing through the air like a billowing cloud of pitch dark silk. In death, however, I cannot say it looks so impressive.

It looked rather like a slimy, rumpled black sack. It reminded me of a cow's afterbirth, and I confess I gagged as I stretched it out on the table.

When flat, it was as large as a single bedsheet and similarly proportioned, though rounder at the edges. I cut the membrane carefully down its side and parted it, opening it up like a thin book. Within, slippery purple organs remained, strangely shallow but clearly what one could expect from a living creature—a heart, kidneys, even primitive lungs of a sort. But there was one organ that stood out from the rest.

It was no larger than a chestnut, perfectly round and sitting at what would have been the Enenra's center. Yet that was not what made it stand out. It was the symbol that adorned it, as if it had been painted there. It was almost invisible, for the symbol was a dark gray. But it was not a spell I recognized.

Again, I have furthered Hominum's knowledge. I wondered if this spell could change the fate of the war. Was it the source of the Enenra's flight, perhaps?

I could not resist. I etched the symbol in the air, my mouth dry, heart pounding. It was a complex symbol—it took me a few tries before the spell would fix to my finger.

Then, I pushed a dribble of mana through.

It was a strange sight. Darkness spread from my fingertip, flowing like black water around the room. Fascinated, I allowed more mana through, until I was drained of all.

Even the stuttering candle on my bedpost could not resist the shadow's insistent advance. Soon, the room was so dark that I could barely see the glowing symbol, even when I held it up to my face.

Now I knew how the orcs had reached the trenches unseen. A powerful spell indeed.

Day 340

Lord Etherington is pleased with my progress, but he insists I focus on discovering the orc keys. I asked him how I can be expected to do that, stuck here on the front lines.

I think my question annoyed him, because he summoned my commanding officer, Captain Bambridge, to his tent. There, he instructed the captain that I was to accompany the next mission behind enemy lines, no matter how dangerous, and particularly if it is one that is likely to encounter the orcs.

I cannot exactly say no, but this feels even more dangerous than if I hadn't accepted Lord Etherington's offer at all!

It seems we rarely actually attack the orcs, and the picture Lord Etherington painted me of commoner second lieutenants being sent into battle over and over were greatly exaggerated.

But I cannot just quit.

I had not given it much thought when I joined the academy, but I remember now signing papers that inducted me into the army when I was given Sable. I had been so overjoyed at receiving her that I did not give it a second glance.

That was when I sold my soul. The army owned me, now and forever.

If I were to leave, it would be desertion. Short of faking my own death, there seems no way out. Perhaps I can gain a position as a teacher at the academy . . . or an assistant perhaps?

I shall write to Provost Scipio and ask him.

Day 345

Provost Scipio's reply is kind but firm. It seems I am not the first graduate to request to teach at the academy—often they are scared of their new positions in the army. He tells me they rotate teachers often, for their roles are coveted by most summoners. In fact, Lord Cavendish and Lady Sinclair will be leaving at the end of this year.

So, I must do my time on the front lines before he would even consider it. And, he rebuked me gently, I am even younger than most students. It just isn't possible.

Day 353

More demon dissections, but nothing new to report. Just added stink in my room and blood under my fingernails. I got lucky with the Enenra. After all, Electra has been dissecting every demon under the sun for years. Never mind. Onward!

Day 367

I inspected another hut, found among the burned trees from when we moved up the trenches. This one was more of a temporary shelter than a permanent living space, perhaps belonging to an orc scout watching our positions. Somehow, the fire only singed the outside. There were orc runes scratched on the walls within, which I took some pleasure in translating. I am quite pleased with how I did it.

You see, when King Corwin arrived here all those years ago, he initially had a peace treaty with the orcs. That treaty, a lengthy, flowery diatribe, was recorded in *both* languages, with phonetic pronunciations scrawled beneath the orcish runes. I was able to dig up a copy in the library's mustiest archives a while back—though Lord Etherington had to send a Shrike demon to bring it to me yesterday. It is likely where the treatise I found on orc phonetics (that I used to name the Akhlut) came from.

Sadly, not all the words were translatable, but what I managed appeared to be a poem, or perhaps a song, about an orcish maiden. It was quite rude, truth be told. Lord Etherington was *not* amused.

Day 382

I went into the jungles tonight. I write this with a shaking hand just minutes after my return. It terrified me to my core.

Lord Etherington cares not a jot for my survival. I bet he already has another errand boy being trained up somewhere, ready to fill my place when I fall.

I was summoned in the darkest of night by Captain Bambridge, and I was ordered to rouse my platoon. An orc had been seen crouched in the darkness of the jungle's edge, spotted by an enterprising young captain who was testing the cat's-eye spell.

We were ordered to attempt to capture it, and I could tell by the reluctance in Bambridge's voice that he did not agree with this order. It must have come from Lord Etherington directly.

My men, who had so often complained about latrine duty, likely now wanted to do nothing else but go back to filling in the stinking troughs.

I decided speed would be of the essence. So we lined up behind the trench, and at my order, we charged across the blackened landscape.

As I ran ahead, my men panicked. Shots whistled over my head as they fired early. I had no choice but to dive to the ground as musket balls whipped past my ears.

I charged again as they stopped to reload, Sable zooming ahead of me, her better eyesight giving her the advantage. I stumbled to the edge, my sword drawn, but it was too late. I flared up a wyrdlight and saw the orc had died, a lucky musket ball lodged somewhere in its skull. I was relieved. What was I thinking, charging alone against a foe in his own territory? Had my men not fired in their panic, I would likely be dead by now, smashed by the orc club that lay beside the corpse.

It took some convincing for the men to come to the jungle edge, but eventually they came to join me and we dragged it back to the front lines.

Men cheered our courage as we came back into view, dragging our prize behind us.

"Our lieutenant's a nutter!" called one of my men. "Charged an orc on 'is own, tried to capture the bleedin' thing."

I think some of the other soldiers thought I had killed it myself, and I am shamed to say I did not correct them.

Men clapped me on the back, applauding my bravery, but the effect was slightly spoiled as I heaved the contents of my stomach onto my boots. Still, it was interesting to see a real orc in the flesh for the first time.

It was a giant at over seven feet tall, proportionally human but with a strange topknot braid and two tusks jutting from its lips. It was an ugly thing, adorned with bone piercings and body paint. Only a grass skirt protected its modesty.

I ordered my men to bury it and retreated to my tent before I voided my stomach once more.

Is it strange that I feel only shame as I write this? Shame and fear.

I need to get away from here.

Day 383

Lord Etherington berated me for killing the orc. I reminded him that no orc had ever been captured and that the attack had been foolhardy at best, but this only seemed to make him more angry.

He was desperate for the orc keys; that is more than obvious. We are losing the war. The cost of keeping so many men here is bankrupting the kingdom, and our men are cowards. They run at the first sign of trouble, so he said.

As he shouted, he paced back and forth in the room, muttering to himself like a madman. This is the man I have entrusted with my life?

I left without being dismissed, and he barely noticed. Just kept muttering to himself.

Lord Cavendish. If only I had listened.

Day 407

I want to succeed. It is easy to forget my parents and friends back home, here on the front lines. If we lost the war and the orcs broke through, my town would be one of the first to be slaughtered. So I will do my duty, just as these other soldiers are doing.

Even if Lord Etherington puts me at risk. It will show them all that I *am* worth something. They'll owe me then.

Day 412

As a fighter, I am near useless to the army. That is clear to me now. Their strength lies in their muskets and their battlemages, not untrained weaklings such as I. It is my mind that is my true talent.

But here, I rot away. Yes, I have made progress . . . but if I let Lord Etherington's mad schemes kill me, it will go to waste. What I need is somewhere safe to continue my research. Oh, to be back in the library, soaking up the knowledge of a millennium.

If I have a chance to go into the jungles, I shall take it. My family still needs me, and the orc keys could change the fate of the war. But at the same time, if there is another place where my skills would be better put to use, then that is where I should go.

I have written to Electra, asking where there might be other writings to study. Perhaps, if I am lucky, I can convince Lord Etherington to send me there.

Day 413

Electra's reply is both exhilarating and disappointing. There is but one place that holds knowledge of summoning. Ancient scrolls, even older than our own! Hundreds of them, if the rumors are true.

But where are they? With the ELVES!

We are not on good terms with the elves. They will not pay the taxes we demand to keep their southern borders safe, so we declared war on them. It was a stupid reaction, because we now need even *more* men to defend our border to the north.

Still, I am preparing my arguments to be allowed to go there. I have set up a time to speak with Lord Etherington tomorrow.

Day 414

Lord Etherington laughed in my face. He said I am becoming complacent, that I need a reminder of why I am here. He told me to fetch Captain Bambridge to him after our meeting, but did not say why. He only smiled at me, and I saw that same, mad look in his eye.

In other news, I hear that our trenches are to be moved up once more, perhaps in a few weeks. More digging for us.

Day 436

They found something while deepening the trenches to the east of us just in case the orcs counterattack when the trenches are moved forward. It's an old camp full of bones, perhaps hundreds of years old. I shall investigate further soon. For now, they are finishing their digging and are not to be disturbed.

Day 439

It is now a year to the day since Lord Etherington ordered my research to begin; yet I am no closer to discovering a new way into the ether. The pentacles the orc shamans use have different keys from ours, of that I am certain now.

Yet they cover their tracks with surprising regularity. I am yet to re-create them with success, but I am sure that should I venture into terrain unmolested by Hominum's touch, clues to what they are may be found. I must therefore make every effort to advance beyond the front lines, where I might see an orc perform a summoning and perhaps catch a glimpse of their pentacle. It is essential we discover which keys they use and in what order.

Today my search finally bore fruit, but not the kind I had hoped for. In my digs at the remains of an old orc encampment, I discovered an incantation, etched on a scroll made of human skin. I have found a surprising joy in its translation; the orc language is brutalist in its expression, but there is an untamed beauty to it that I cannot explain.

I suspect the scroll imparts a demon to the adept who reads it. In all likelihood this demon will be a low-level imp gifted from an older shaman to his apprentice to start him in the learning of the dark art. This will be a rare opportunity to examine a demon from a different part of the ether. Perhaps through more careful scrutiny, this imp will point me in the right direction. With each failure, my resolve grows, yet I cannot shake the feeling that my mission is perceived by my colleagues as a fool's errand. Though my demon is weak, I will prove to the naysayers that I have just as much right to be an officer as those of noble blood.

Now I must away, for my commanding officer has called me to his tent. Perhaps this will be my first opportunity to cross into enemy territory.

Treatise on the Basics of Summoning

by James Baker

The ability to summon is passed down through the blood. The firstborn child always inherits the gift, while their younger siblings have a much smaller chance.

Every summoner must at first be gifted a demon through the reading aloud of a summoning scroll, usually through a parent or sponsor. Once summoned, the demons act as familiars and share a mental and emotional connection with their human counterparts. Without a demon, a summoner would be almost indistinguishable from a normal person, although some exhibit the early ability to produce small sparks or flames. The source of their true power is the channeling of mana from their demons.

Demons can be infused within their summoner when they are not needed, allowing them to recover their mana and rest. While within, the demon can see all that the summoner does. In order to be summoned or infused, the demon must be standing upon a pentacle, which must be comprised of or inscribed on organic material. A summoner must power up the pentacle with mana before the summoning or infusion may occur.

Demons are captured from a disk-shaped world called the ether. Around the edge of this world is an abyss, where warped, tentacled demons known as Ceteans live. The outer rim is made of a Mars-like desert called the deadlands, followed by jungles, seas, mountains and volcanoes as you come closer to the center, where most of the demons can be found.

The ether is accessed by a keyed pentacle, differing from the pentacle needed for summoning in that it has symbols on each point of the star, acting as coordinates for an approximate location in the ether. This portal must be fueled with mana at all times to keep it open. Summoners are unable to enter the ether unless wearing a suit, not unlike a deep-sea diver's, as the air is poisonous. They will usually use their demons to hunt for others in the ether, dragging them back through the portal so their summoner can infuse them and thus capture them.

Summoners are able to use scrying crystals to see and hear what their demons do while they are in the ether—all scrying crystals are made from corundum crystal. Corundum crystal is also used in charging stones, a column made up of crystals of the same color.

Demonic species come in all shapes and sizes, from small beetle demons known as Mites to larger ones, such as Griffins and Wendigos. The demons will also have a fixed amount of mana and a level, depending on their species. Summoners also have levels, which improve as time goes by and they become more experienced. The more powerful a summoner, the higher the level of demon they are capable of summoning. For example, a level-ten summoner could own ten Mites, which are level one, or one Minotaur, which is level ten.

Finally, there are the spells. To perform a spell, a summoner must etch a symbol in the air with a glowing finger, leaving a blue glyph that will eventually "fix" and follow their fingertip as if attached by an invisible frame. Only when the mana is channeled through this glyph does it become a spell.

A note from Dame Fairhaven

That was the last entry in Baker's diary. I mourned for the boy when Fletcher Raleigh first brought this to me, for he was a kindhearted soul. I only wish I had known what he was going through at the time. I hope that no other child under my care will ever feel such loneliness as he did. Was I blind to the bullying? Or did I not want to see?

I have asked Fletcher to recount what Sergeant Rotherham told him of Baker's final moments, which I have transcribed here below. I wanted to ask the sergeant myself, but tragically, this is not possible anymore. Fletcher has done his best to keep the story as close to verbatim as possible, but memory is a fickle thing. This is the best he could do.

"Their orders were to scout out the next forward line. The trenches were advancing again. It was darker than a stack of black cats that night, barely a sliver of a moon to light their way. Apparently they made more noise than a rhino charging as they made their way through the thickets, and it was a miracle they made it more than ten minutes without being noticed.

"Baker led the way, because his demon had good night vision. It didn't help much, but it kept them in the right direction, even if they kept tripping and nearly firing their muskets. Rotherham thought it was a suicide mission—a way of getting the older soldiers off the king's pay.

"Eventually they became lost, as the few stars that Baker had been using to navigate became covered by rain clouds. This compounded the soldiers' predicament: Muskets won't fire with wet gunpowder.

"They were ambushed soon after the rain. Javelins

whistled through the trees and plucked men from the earth as if the world had flipped sideways. They didn't even see their attackers, but half the platoon was dead in the first volley, and Rotherham was already running before the second. Baker led the retreat, following the chirps of his demon. In the end, Baker collapsed, and Rotherham noticed that he had been winged by a javelin in his side. There was a lot of blood, and Rotherham thought he was a dead man already, but the demon wouldn't leave without him. Rotherham carried him the rest of the way.

"Rotherham took his pack, knowing Baker wouldn't need it anymore. I'm not sure what happened after that, only that the demon stayed by Baker's side and refused to leave it for some time."

It was this last point that gave me pause. You see (and this next part is for the novices reading), when a summoner dies, their demon fades into the ether. Usually, they do not hang around for long, unless they have some special task to perform, in which case they resist the ether's call. But this demon stayed, and for a while it seems. Why?

So, I investigated further. Unfortunately, Lord Etherington died in the Battle of Vocans, so I could not speak to him directly. Instead, I spoke to the soldiers in Lord Etherington's battalion, and Captain Bambridge.

Yet no matter how many men I spoke to, not a single one could remember what had happened to Baker's body. Nobody buried him. It was as if the morning came, and then they moved the trenches up, charging the jungle once more and burning their way forward. In the chaos of it all, Baker's body disappeared. One assumed that some kind soul had taken it upon themselves to bury the boy, perhaps a friend of his.

But this wasn't enough for me. And there was something else too. When I interviewed Fletcher at his home in Raleighshire, he was being visited by his elven friend Sylva. In fact, it seems the two are working closely together; she is always there when I visit the gremlins (they have become my latest area of study—there is almost nothing in our archives about them!). It took me several visits to Raleightown to catch Fletcher for an interview, truth be told, as they are always flying off on Sylva's Griffin, scouting the jungles for signs of orc attacks. They are so diligent, sometimes they don't return until the dead of night. I only wish I had their work ethic.

In any case, when I was telling Fletcher about my progress with Baker's journal, Sylva's eyes lit up with what seemed to me an unusual interest. She clung to my every word.

So, after my interview, I took her aside and asked her, quite plainly, what she was hiding. She was flustered, but seemed to calm when I asked her again what she knew of Baker. She thought for a moment, then shrugged and told me all. The war was practically over, she said, so telling me couldn't do any harm.

You see . . . when Sylva arrived at Vocans, she was already able to infuse her demon on her own. She had knowledge of many things she should not have, but claimed she had learned them from ancient elven books. I believed her. But . . . as it turns out . . . she had a tutor.

James Baker did not die on that godforsaken mission. Somehow he survived and made his way in secret to the Great Forest. There, he offered his services to the elves in exchange for sanctuary and access to their most ancient of books. Sylva kept his secret all these years, even from her

closest friends, for she knew he would face charges of desertion and be summarily executed if he were to be found out.

You may be wondering why I am outing James in
this way. Well, King Harold has offered him a full
pardon, thanks, in no small part, to the fact that over the
years he has sent dozens of anonymous letters to Electra,
helping her advance Hominum's summoning research. He
called himself Captain Jacoby in his messages and delivered them through his Chamrosh in the dead of night.
Sylva confirmed that Baker did indeed increase in level
and capture a Chamrosh, though he kept his Mite as well.
At no point did Electra know Baker's true identity, but it
was he who identified the *Medusa*, *Stheno* and *Euryale*
plants, as well as sharing spells such as the ethereal blade,
among others. A dozen new demons were also added to
Vocans's official demonology.

I have written to Baker in the hopes that someday he
will come back to Vocans and take over as librarian when I
retire. No reply as of yet. But I live in hope.

Thank you for reading.

Yours faithfully,

Dame Fairhaven

THE DEMONOLOGY CODEX

*The complete
Demonology Codex,
compiled by James Baker
and updated
by Major Goodwin
of Vocans Academy*

This demon is one of the most common prey animals in the ether and is not a popular choice among summoners. It appears as a hare with a pair of antlers on its forehead. Known for its speed and sharp incisors, this demon can still hold its own in a fight, although it is more likely to flee unless cornered.

CLASSIFICATION: *Caprids*

BASE MANA LEVEL: 6

MANA ABILITIES: None

NATURAL SKILLS:
Acute Hearing, Agility

RARITY: Very Common

DIET: Herbivore

ATTACK/DEFENSE:
1. Antlers, 2. Bite

Lesser Mites are the most common demon in Hominum's part of the ether and are the food source of many demonic species. They are usually around the same size and appearance as the beetles one finds in Hominum. This similarity in appearance has allowed some summoners, both orc and human, to spy on their enemies undetected. However, using up an entire summoning level on such a weak demon is considered wasteful by most.

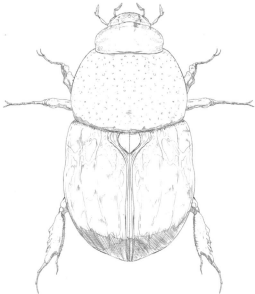

Classification: *Arthropidae*

BASE MANA LEVEL: 6	RARITY: Very Common
MANA ABILITIES: None	DIET: Omnivore
NATURAL SKILLS: Flying	ATTACK/DEFENSE: 1. Mandibles

Though there are several species of smaller, insect-like Mites, Scarab Mites are the most powerful of the Mite genus. These demons appear as large flying beetles and vary from dull brown to brightly colored. When full grown, a Scarab develops a weapon to complement its powerful mandibles—a nasty stinger, which can temporarily paralyze its enemy. Many summoners use Mites as scouts to explore the ether before sending a more powerful demon in to hunt.

Classification: *Arthropidae*

BASE MANA LEVEL: 7

MANA ABILITIES: None

NATURAL SKILLS: Flying

DIET: Omnivore

RARITY: Very Common

ATTACK/DEFENSE: 1. Mandibles, 2. Paralytic Sting

This elemental demon appears as a glowing globe of blue, much like a wyrdlight. Though beautiful to look at, they are treacherous, leading any that might follow into the pits of sinking sand within their native swamplands. Once the victim is stuck fast or drowned, nearby Will-o'-the-wisps will flock together and drain it of its blood. Beneath the glow of blue, they appear rather like limbless glowworms.

Classification: *Elemental*

BASE MANA LEVEL: 10

MANA ABILITIES: Blood Drain

NATURAL SKILLS: Flying

RARITY: Common

DIET: Carnivore

ATTACK/DEFENSE: 1. Wyrdlight Flash

The Lavellan is a ratlike demon armed with two venomous fangs where its incisors should be and a thick, wormlike tail. Though it's a solid starter demon, many summoners turn their noses up at using the Lavellan thanks to its verminous appearance. Unlike a Mite's or Damsel's, the Lavellan's venom acts much like a snake's, causing excruciating pain and eventual death unless antivenom is administered. Since so many shamans use them as demons, it is suspected that at least some of the orc part of the ether is made up of swampland, for that is the Lavellan's preferred habitat.

Classification: *Rodentia*

BASE MANA LEVEL: 13

MANA ABILITIES: None

NATURAL SKILLS: Climbing

RARITY: Common

DIET: Omnivore

ATTACK/DEFENSE: 1. Poison Fangs

This demon appears in the shape of a lizard, but with the body parts of an insect—as if made from a beetle's carapace with the same segmented joints. Its wings, though shaped like a Wyvern's, are made from the same fragile material as a butterfly's. The demon is prized for its ability to change color at will to blend in with its environment like a chameleon. Along with its potent sting, the demon's insect-like eyes and antennae allow it to sense heat and movement, giving the summoner a new perspective when scrying.

Classification: *Arthropidae, Reptilia*

BASE MANA LEVEL: 17

MANA ABILITIES: None

NATURAL SKILLS: Flying, Color Change, Heat Vision, Sonar

RARITY: Endangered

DIET: Omnivore

ATTACK/DEFENSE:

1. Paralytic Sting

BAKU—LEVEL 3

The Baku shares many similarities in appearance and body shape with a real-world creature known as a tapir. The Baku is a prey animal in the ether and is not considered a suitable demon for summoners. It can be described as a pig-sized demon with an elephantine trunk and tusks and the striped orange fur of a tiger.

Classification: *Megafauns*

BASE MANA LEVEL: 20

MANA ABILITIES: None

NATURAL SKILLS:
Prehensile Trunk

RARITY: Uncommon

DIET: Herbivore

ATTACK/DEFENSE:
1. Tusks, 2. Trunk

An insect-like demon akin to a giant dragonfly, with an iridescent carapace and four wings. These deceptively fast creatures are highly maneuverable in the air, capable of changing direction on a penny. They are a close cousin to the Mite, with a sting that is three times as potent. These demons are common throughout the known ether.

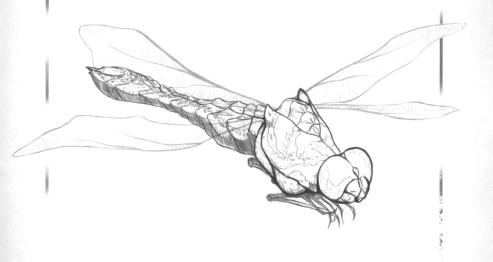

Classification: *Arthropidae*

BASE MANA LEVEL: 21

MANA ABILITIES: None

NATURAL SKILLS: Flying, Agility

RARITY: Very Common

DIET: Herbivore

ATTACK/DEFENSE: 1. Paralytic Sting

A demon that appears similar to a large fanged weasel, with serrated bone-blades replacing its paws. Relatively common in the orcish part of the ether, these expendable demons are regular attackers of Hominum's front lines.

Classification: *Rodentia*

BASE MANA LEVEL: 20

MANA ABILITIES: None

NATURAL SKILLS: Climbing

RARITY: Common

DIET: Omnivore

ATTACK/DEFENSE: 1. Bone Claws, 2. Bite

The Kappa is one of the more common Aquarine demons. Appearing as an overgrown toad with a turtle's beak and shell, this demon's most unusual feature is the hollow indentation at the top of its head. It is theorized that this bowl is used to store water when the Kappa travels overland, allowing it to breathe with the Kappa's large gill at the bottom. Other than its shell, this demon is a weak species and serves as a prey animal to the Nanaues and Akhluts of the ether's oceans.

Classification: *Aquarine, Reptilia*

BASE MANA LEVEL: 21	RARITY: Uncommon
MANA ABILITIES: None	DIET: Omnivore
NATURAL SKILLS: Amphibious	ATTACK/DEFENSE: 1. Beak, 2. Shell

The Bildad is a rare amphibious creature that shares some similarities to a platypus in that it has the appearance of a strange amalgamation of disparate creatures. One might describe it as having a hybrid anatomy of a sparrow's head, kangaroo legs, a flat beaver tail and webbed, frog-like feet. It has a set of spurs on its hind feet that it uses to inject venom considered three times as potent as a Scarab Mite's.

Classification: *Rodentia, Aves*

BASE MANA LEVEL: 29	RARITY: Rare
MANA ABILITIES: None	DIET: Omnivore
NATURAL SKILLS: Amphibious, Jumping	ATTACK/DEFENSE: 1. Paralytic Spurs

The Coatl is a serpent with multicolored plumage instead of scales. Although not capable of flight, the Coatl uses its feathers to glide down from the ether's trees and onto unsuspecting prey below. The Coatl will use its venom to paralyze a victim and then constrict it to death, before swallowing the carcass whole.

Classification: *Reptilia, Aves*

BASE MANA LEVEL: 28	RARITY: Uncommon
MANA ABILITIES: None	DIET: Carnivore
NATURAL SKILLS: Gliding	ATTACK/DEFENSE: 1. Poison Fangs, 2. Constriction

This demon is the gentler cousin to the Manticore and Chimera. It has the body of a lion and the head of a ram, complete with curling horns and beard. However, it is as small as a billy goat, and the claws are not as large or sharp as other Felidae demons.

Classification: *Felidae, Caprids*

BASE MANA LEVEL: 27

MANA ABILITIES: None

NATURAL SKILLS: Agility

RARITY: Uncommon

DIET: Herbivore

ATTACK/DEFENSE:

1. Claws, 2. Horns

GRYPHOWL—LEVEL 4

This demon is a combination of cat and owl and is closely related to the Griffin and Chamrosh, though it is far rarer. Their sharp retractable claws and beak are their best weapons, but it is their keen intelligence and agility in the air that makes them such a desirable demon. The Gryphowl is a loner by nature but will often form a close bond with its summoner and fellow demons if treated well.

Classification: *Aves, Felidae*

BASE MANA LEVEL: 30

MANA ABILITIES: None

NATURAL SKILLS: Flying, Climbing, Eyesight

RARITY: Rare

DIET: Carnivore

ATTACK/DEFENSE:

1. Beak, 2. Claws

This demon is relatively common in the ether and is considered an acquired taste by some summoners. It appears similar to a bear-sized wombat, with a pair of small antlers on its head. Its claws, teeth and horns are not particularly sharp, but the demon's size and muscle more than make up for this shortfall.

Classification: *Megafauns*

BASE MANA LEVEL: 27

MANA ABILITIES: None

NATURAL SKILLS: Digging

RARITY: Common

DIET: Herbivore

ATTACK/DEFENSE:

1. Bite, 2. Scratch, 3. Antlers

This dog-sized demon appears very similar to an overgrown otter, with a tail spiked like a morning star and two large incisors. They are often found in the lakes and rivers of the ether, as they are especially fond of swimming.

Classification: *Rodentia*

BASE MANA LEVEL: 24

MANA ABILITIES: None

NATURAL SKILLS: Swimming

RARITY: Common

DIET: Omnivore

ATTACK/DEFENSE:
1. Spiked Tail, 2. Buckteeth

The Ropen appears as a hybrid between bat and bird. It has no feathers; its wings are made from a stretched membrane between clawed wing joints. When hunting, it uses its powerful talons to snatch smaller prey. Its most birdlike appendages are a long pelican beak and an elongated crest on the back of its head.

Classification: *Reptilia, Aves*

BASE MANA LEVEL: 27

MANA ABILITIES: None

NATURAL SKILLS: Flying

RARITY: Common

DIET: Carnivore

ATTACK/DEFENSE: 1. Beak,
2. Talons

These birdlike demons migrate annually across Hominum's part of the ether, making entry extremely dangerous for one week of the year. They are known for their long black feathers, and their wingspan is as wide as a man is tall, with each wing's endmost feathers tipped with bleached white. A Shrike's beak is hooked, and it has a bright red wattle underneath its neck and a red ridge along the top of its head like that of a rooster.

Classification: *Aves*

BASE MANA LEVEL: 25	RARITY: Migratory
MANA ABILITIES: None	DIET: Carnivore
NATURAL SKILLS: Flying	ATTACK/DEFENSE: 1. Beak, 2. Talons

Often mistaken for the Gryphowl, the Strix appears as an owl-ish bird with four limbs. Their feathers are tipped with red, giving them a fearsome appearance. They are common in known parts of the ether but are rarely captured due to their vicious nature. It is not unknown for a Strix to kill and eat its siblings when they reach maturity.

Classification: *Aves*

BASE MANA LEVEL: 25

MANA ABILITIES: None

NATURAL SKILLS: Flying

RARITY: Migratory

DIET: Carnivore

ATTACK/DEFENSE:

1. Beak, 2. Talons

Veos could be described as a cross between armadillos and hedgehogs. Covered in armored plating, the Veo is able to roll into a ball to keep itself protected. Small holes dotted at the intersections of its plates allow this demon to extend spikes from within, adding a second layer of defense. If the Veo wishes to go on the offensive, it is able to throw quills rather like a porcupine, leaving its opponent stuck with barbed spines that are painful to remove.

Classification: *Megafauns*

BASE MANA LEVEL: 28	DIET: Omnivore
MANA ABILITIES: None	ATTACK/DEFENSE:
NATURAL SKILLS: Rolling	1. Armor Plating, 2. Spikes,
RARITY: Rare	3. Quill Throw

Appearing much like an overgrown wasp or bee, these demons are often difficult to capture because of their tendency to travel in swarms. Armed with a stinger just as deadly as a Damsel's and a pair of potent mandibles, these demons are a favorite among orc shamans.

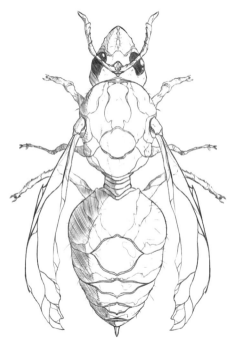

Classification: *Arthropidae*

BASE MANA LEVEL: 28

MANA ABILITIES: None

NATURAL SKILLS: Flying

RARITY: Very Common

DIET: Omnivore

ATTACK/DEFENSE: 1. Paralytic Sting, 2. Mandibles

The Yale is one of the ether's more common demons, but it is rarely captured due to its poor mana levels. It looks something like a hybrid of cow and deer, with cloven feet and a pair of curved horns. A Yale's dark brown fur is striped white and black along its spine. These demons have the unique ability to manipulate the position of their horns, sometimes spinning them like a pair of drills when charging an opponent, be that another male during mating season or one of their many predators.

Classification: *Caprids*

BASE MANA LEVEL: 22	RARITY: Very Common
MANA ABILITIES: None	DIET: Herbivore
NATURAL SKILLS: Agility	ATTACK/DEFENSE: 1. Horns

The Catoblepas has a powerful bovine body and horns, a horse's mane and a head similar to that of a warthog. This herbivorous demon has a penchant for eating poisonous plants, leaving its breath toxic. Although immune to their own Catoblepases' noxious fumes, summoners avoid this demon for fear of inadvertently injuring others. These demons are one of the more dangerous prey animals that the ether's larger carnivores feed upon.

Classification: *Caprids*

BASE MANA LEVEL: 35

MANA ABILITIES: None

NATURAL SKILLS:
Immunity to Poison

RARITY: Rare

DIET: Herbivore

ATTACK/DEFENSE: 1. Toxic Breath, 2. Horns, 3. Tusks

CHAMROSH—LEVEL 5

This hawk-dog hybrid is a quarter of the size of its closest cousin, the Griffin. The Chamrosh is renowned for its loyal and loving nature and will often become lonely when separated from its master. As the preferred support demon of the Celestial Corps, this demon is a favorite among summoners.

Classification: *Aves, Canidae*

BASE MANA LEVEL: 35

MANA ABILITIES: None

NATURAL SKILLS: Flying, Eyesight

RARITY: Uncommon

DIET: Carnivore

ATTACK/DEFENSE: 1. Beak

The Cockatrice appears as a large, rooster-shaped lizard with a long tail. Its body is covered in scales, with a smattering of fiery feathers along its limbs, tail and spine. Though they have short forearms, the large raptor talons on their feet and powerful back legs make them a dangerous predator. Even their mouths are formidable, with a short beak on the end of a tooth-filled muzzle.

Classification: *Aves, Reptilia*

BASE MANA LEVEL: 33	RARITY: Rare
MANA ABILITIES: None	DIET: Carnivore
NATURAL SKILLS: Agility	ATTACK/DEFENSE: 1. Talons, 2. Beak

The Encantado is a four-limbed dolphin-like demon, native to the waters of the ether. Though the webbed claws of their fore-legs and hind legs are not particularly sharp, they use their hard skulls and powerful fluked tails to batter their enemies aside. If an Encantado has recently been swimming, it is not unknown for it to spray water from its blowhole to blind its enemies. They are sought after for their fierce intellect, playful nature and speed, since they are faster than both the Nanaue and Akhlut. Unfortunately, they only appear occasionally in Hominum's part of the ether when swimming up one of the few rivers in the area.

Classification: *Aquarine*

BASE MANA LEVEL: 38

MANA ABILITIES: None

NATURAL SKILLS: Swimming, Jumping

RARITY: Rare

DIET: Carnivore

ATTACK/DEFENSE: 1. Claws, 2. Head Butt, 3. Spray

ENFIELD—LEVEL 5

The Enfield is both rarer and smaller than its cousin, the Vulpid, and is the size of a large dog. It has the head of a fox, forelegs of an eagle, the narrow chest of a greyhound and the hindquarters of a wolf. Its front talons are dangerously sharp, and it has tawny brown feathers interspersed among the red fur of its front and the gray of its back.

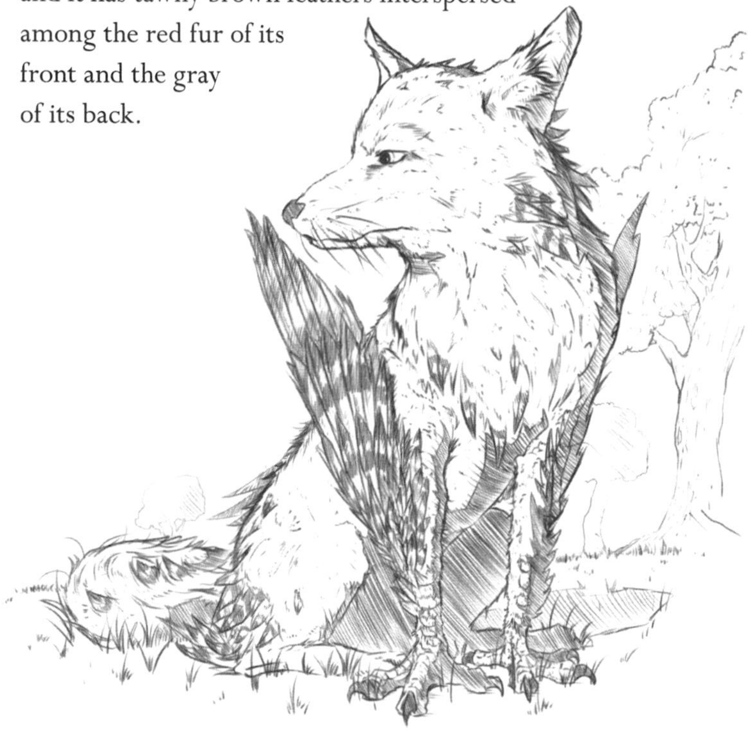

Classification: *Aves*, *Canidae*

BASE MANA LEVEL: 35
MANA ABILITIES: None
NATURAL SKILLS: Acute Scent, Acute Hearing, Agility

RARITY: Rare
DIET: Carnivore
ATTACK/DEFENSE: 1. Bite, 2. Talons

These demons are native to the waters of the ether. They appear as scaled horses, with barbed fins on their forelegs and a fishlike tail replacing their hindquarters. Though beautiful, these demons are carnivorous predators, leaping from the surface to snag prey with their barbs and drowning them underwater. Given their incompatibility with land, Kelpies are not popular among shamans and summoners alike.

Classification: *Equine, Reptilia*

BASE MANA LEVEL: 38

MANA ABILITIES: None

NATURAL SKILLS: Swimming, Agility

RARITY: Uncommon

DIET: Carnivore

ATTACK/DEFENSE: 1. Barbed Fins

The Leucrotta is a zebra-striped demon that prefers to hunt at dusk. It is an unusual creature with cloven hooves, a lionlike tail and the head and body shape of an overgrown badger. It is not unknown for this demon to follow Shrike migrations across the ether, eating the carrion left behind. These solitary demons were once popular with Hominum's summoners but have since fallen out of favor.

Classification: *Megafauns*

BASE MANA LEVEL: 33

MANA ABILITIES: None

NATURAL SKILLS: Night Vision

RARITY: Uncommon

DIET: Carnivore

ATTACK/DEFENSE: 1. Bite

MUSIMON—LEVEL 5

The Musimon appears as a cross between a horse and an enormous, bearded billy goat, with two pairs of horns on its head. The lower pair is curled and thick, while the higher pair is long and sharp like a bull's. These demons are popular among the Dragoons, especially for the newer, less powerful summoners.

Classification: *Caprids, Equine*

BASE MANA LEVEL: 30

MANA ABILITIES: None

NATURAL SKILLS: Jumping

RARITY: Common

DIET: Herbivore

ATTACK/DEFENSE: 1. Horns, 2. Kick

RAIJU—LEVEL 5

The Raiju is so rare that only five have ever been captured in Hominum's history. Appearing much like a hybrid of squirrel, raccoon and mongoose, this mammalian demon has large yellow eyes and dark blue fur that is emblazoned with whorls and jagged stripes of teal. It has unusually high mana levels and at its most powerful, the Raiju's lightning-bolt attack is capable of killing a bull orc. Strangely, this demon prefers to sleep on its summoner's stomach, curling around its master's navel.

Classification: *Rodentia*

BASE MANA LEVEL: 40
MANA ABILITIES: Lightning
NATURAL SKILLS: Climbing,
Immune to Lightning

RARITY: Endangered
DIET: Omnivore
ATTACK/DEFENSE:
1. Lightning Bolt

Salamanders are extremely rare and do not exist in Hominum's part of the ether. Not much is known about their habitat or history, though there is evidence that orcs have captured them in the past. They are the size of a ferret, with a similarly lithe body and limbs long enough to lope rather than scuttle like a lizard. Their skin is the color of dark burgundy, with eyes that are large, amber and round like those of an owl. Salamanders have no teeth to speak of, but their snout ends sharply, almost like a river turtle's beak.

Classification: *Reptilia*

BASE MANA LEVEL: 45

MANA ABILITIES:
Fire Breathing, Healing

NATURAL SKILLS: Immune to Fire, Agility, Climbing

RARITY: Endangered

DIET: Carnivore

ATTACK/DEFENSE: 1. Fire Breath, 2. Tail Spike, 3. Claws, 4. Beak

This demon could be described as an eight-legged horse, sporting four eyes like a Canid or Felid. Known for its powerful musculature, aggressive nature and racing ability, this demon is a popular choice among Hominum's mounted summoners, the Dragoons. With enough stamina to run for days and the speed of a cheetah, these demons are incredibly difficult to capture.

Classification: *Equine*

BASE MANA LEVEL: 35

MANA ABILITIES: None

NATURAL SKILLS: Speed, Stamina

RARITY: Rare

DIET: Herbivore

ATTACK/DEFENSE: 1. Kick

The Arach appears as an enormous spider, almost as large as a wild boar. Its eight dextrous legs are capable of skillful manipulation, allowing the demon to jump as high as ten feet and grasp its opponents by the face. The Arach has three powerful abilities. The first is the gossamer spell, shooting a luminescent web that puts one in mind of the silk of a glowworm—an adhesive that fades out of existence after a few hours. The second is the vicious stinger that protrudes from its abdomen, the venom of which is capable of killing a grown man, if the impalement on the spike does not do the job first. Finally, rather like some breeds of tarantula, the Arach is capable of releasing the bristled hairs from its back to float in the air, scourging its opponents' skin and even blinding them. Only its summoners are immune to these bristles as well as the Arach's venom.

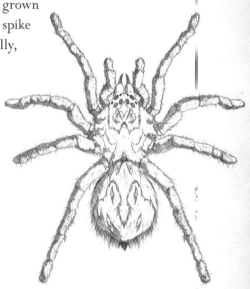

Classification: *Arthropidae*

BASE MANA LEVEL: 45	DIET: Carnivore
MANA ABILITIES: Gossamer	ATTACK/DEFENSE: 1. Bristles,
NATURAL SKILLS: Climbing, Jumping	2. Ethereal Threads,
RARITY: Rare	3. Venomous Sting

This badger-shaped demon has tough skin almost indistinguishable from bark, which it uses to camouflage itself in the jungles of the ether. Although relatively common, their tendency to hide at the top of tree trunks and the ridge of poisonous spines they can shoot from their backs make them difficult to capture. Their diet consists solely of vegetation, which they crush in their ridge-filled mouths.

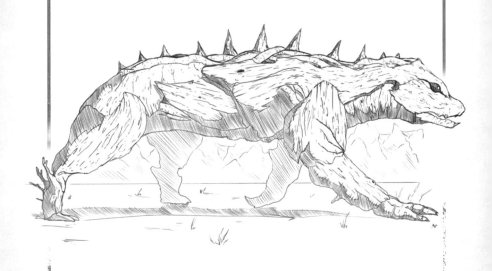

Classification: *Viridae*

BASE MANA LEVEL: 45	RARITY: Average
MANA ABILITIES: None	DIET: Herbivore
NATURAL SKILLS: Camouflage, Spines	ATTACK/DEFENSE: 1. Paralytic Spines, 2. Tough Skin

Close cousin to the Alicorn, this demon bears the front half of a horse and the back half of a cockerel, with a curved beak and red wattle instead of a muzzle. The male Hippalectryon's red and green blend of fur and plumage culminates in a fan of bright tail feathers that it uses to attract its equally deadly, fawn-colored female counterpart. The hooked talons of its hind legs can easily disembowel an attacker, yet that does not prevent a Hippalectryon's higher-level predators from trying to attack. This demon is a favorite among the Dragoons, Hominum's mounted battlemages.

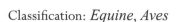

Classification: *Equine, Aves*

BASE MANA LEVEL: 43	RARITY:: Uncommon
MANA ABILITIES: None	DIET: Omnivore
NATURAL SKILLS: None	ATTACK/DEFENSE: 1. Beak, 2. Talons

The Naga is considered one of more unusual-looking demons of the ether. Its lower half is similar to an eel's, yet its upper body is more humanoid, with two arms and a torso. It sports webbed spines around its head and along its vertebrae like a cobra's hood, which it will flare at the first sign of danger. The face is lizard-like, with the barbed whiskers of a catfish and a long, forked tongue. Though amphibious, it is slow on land and lacks offensive capabilities, so most summoners steer clear of them. Their hands are their best tools, which they use to winkle out prey from coral beds or snatch unsuspecting demons from the water's edge.

Classification: *Aquarine, Reptilia*

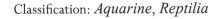

BASE MANA LEVEL: 42

MANA ABILITIES: None

NATURAL SKILLS:
Prehensile Hands

RARITY: Rare

DIET: Omnivore

ATTACK/DEFENSE: 1. Fists,
2. Primitive Tools

The Shrike Matriarch is the maternal leader of a Shrike flock. Almost twice as large as the average Shrike, these demons are not to be underestimated. It is not unknown for a Matriarch to carry off juvenile Canids, should the opportunity present itself.

Classification: *Aves*

BASE MANA LEVEL: 38

MANA ABILITIES: None

NATURAL SKILLS: Flying

RARITY: Migratory

DIET: Carnivore

ATTACK/DEFENSE: 1. Beak, 2. Talons

VULPID—LEVEL 6

A close cousin to the Canid, this slightly smaller, fox-like demon has three tails and is known for its agility and speed.

Classification: *Canidae*

BASE MANA LEVEL: 42

MANA ABILITIES: None

NATURAL SKILLS: Acute Scent, Acute Hearing, Agility

RARITY: Uncommon

DIET: Carnivore

ATTACK/DEFENSE:
1. Bite, 2. Claws

One
of four
elemental
birdlike demons, the
Caladrius is cousin to the
fiery Phoenix, the icy Polarion
and the lightning-powered
Halcyon. With the white feathers
and gentle features of a dove, this
demon's high mana and rare healing
powers are highly desired, even if its relatively small talons are not. These demons are
rumored to spend most of their time high above
the cloudscape of the ether, where the air is too thin
for other demons to find them.

Classification: *Aves*

BASE MANA LEVEL: 52

MANA ABILITIES: Healing

NATURAL SKILLS: Flying

RARITY: Very Rare

DIET: Omnivore

ATTACK/DEFENSE: 1. Healing,
2. Beak

A doglike demon with four eyes, lethal claws, a fox-like tail and a thick ridge of fur down its spine. These demons range in size from that of a large dog to a small pony, depending on the breed.

Classification: *Canidae*

BASE MANA LEVEL: 48	RARITY: Common
MANA ABILITIES: None	DIET: Carnivore
NATURAL SKILLS: Acute Hearing, Acute Smell, Agility	ATTACK/DEFENSE: 1. Bite, 2. Claws

FELID—LEVEL 7

This bipedal cat demon has four eyes and the stature and intelligence of a jungle chimpanzee. Their breeds vary from leonine, tigrine and leopine, bearing resemblances to lions, tigers and leopards respectively.

Classification: *Felidae*

BASE MANA LEVEL: 50	RARITY: Common
MANA ABILITIES: None	DIET: Carnivore
NATURAL SKILLS: Agility, Climbing	ATTACK/DEFENSE: 1. Bite, 2. Claws

The Halcyon is thought to be the most common of the four elemental avians, with bright metallic feathers that make it shine brightly when it flies. With razor-sharp talons, high mana levels and the ability to fire lightning from its elongated tail feathers, its conspicuousness is its only disadvantage.

Classification: *Aves*

BASE MANA LEVEL: 52	RARITY: Very Rare
MANA ABILITIES: Lightning	DIET: Omnivore
NATURAL SKILLS: Flying, Immune to Lightning	ATTACK/DEFENSE: 1. Beak, 2. Lightning, 3. Talons

KIRIN—LEVEL 7

The Kirin might be described as a hybrid between reptile and horse. Though their body shape resembles that of their equine cousins, Kirins are armored from head to hoof in viridian scales. Much like its cousin the Alicorn, the Kirin sports a horn in the center of its forehead, though the Kirin's branches in two rather like an antler. Vainglorious summoners actively seek out this rare demon, as their lustrous red manes and tails make for a regal mount. It is a favorite among Dragoon officers.

Classification: *Equine, Reptilia*

BASE MANA LEVEL: 50

MANA ABILITIES: None

NATURAL SKILLS: None

RARITY: Rare

DIET: Omnivore

ATTACK/DEFENSE: 1. Armor, 2. Horn

PHOENIX—LEVEL 7

A large bird with red-orange plumage and long tail feathers like that of a peacock, the Phoenix is the rarest of the four elemental avian demons. High in mana and capable of breathing fire like a Salamander, these demons are said to inhabit the rims of active volcanoes in the ether.

Classification: *Aves*

BASE MANA LEVEL: 52

MANA ABILITIES: Flames, Immune to Fire

NATURAL SKILLS: Flying

RARITY: Very Rare

DIET: Omnivore

ATTACK/DEFENSE: 1. Beak, 2. Flames, 3. Talons

Polarions are believed to inhabit the clouds above the ether's seas, using their frost ability to hunt any small demons foolish enough to leap out of the water. Rare sightings report the demon to be built much like a kingfisher, with blue-black plumage and a white belly. They are unusually high in mana and have the extremely rare ability to freeze their enemies, making them a fine addition to any summoner's roster.

Classification: *Aves*

BASE MANA LEVEL: 52

MANA ABILITIES: Frost, Immune to Frost

NATURAL SKILLS: Flying

RARITY: Very Rare

DIET: Omnivore

ATTACK/DEFENSE: 1. Beak, 2. Frost, 3. Talons

A horse demon with swanlike wings and a single horn growing from the center of its forehead. These equine demons are notoriously difficult to capture thanks to their speed both in the air and on land. The Alicorn herds migrate across Hominum's part of the ether once each decade, and those that are slow enough to be captured tend to be the sick, injured or young.

Classification: *Aves, Caprids, Equine*

BASE MANA LEVEL: 56

MANA ABILITIES: None

NATURAL SKILLS: Flying, Agility

RARITY: Migratory

DIET: Herbivore

ATTACK/DEFENSE: 1. Horn, 2. Kick

This rare demon stands on two legs and has the head of a jackal. Though their bodies are rangy and gaunt, they are known for their agility and speed. Unusual for demons related to the common Canid, this demon has only two eyes.

Classification: *Canidae*

BASE MANA LEVEL: 53

MANA ABILITIES: None

NATURAL SKILLS: Acute Smell, Acute Hearing, Agility

RARITY: Very Rare

DIET: Carnivore

ATTACK/DEFENSE: 1. Bite, 2. Claws

The Dryad is one of the few demons in the Viridae family. These treelike beings are roughly humanoid, roaming the forests in search of fertile soil to root their feet in. Varying in size dependent on age, the Dryad grows from a small, green shoot to the height and breadth of an old oak. This process takes almost a century, and most Dryads are eaten before they reach full maturity. However, adolescent Dryads have a thick layer of bark to protect them. Their horny fists, paired with their ability to regrow limbs and damaged tissue, make them a force to be reckoned with. Though they are not endangered, few Dryads are ever seen, thanks to their ability to blend with the vegetation around them.

Classification: *Viridae*

BASE MANA LEVEL: 56
MANA ABILITIES: Healing, Regrowth
NATURAL SKILLS: Tough Skin
RARITY: Very Rare

DIET: Herbivore
ATTACK/DEFENSE:
1. Tough Skin, 2. Regrowth,
3. Fists

The Enenra appears as a floating haze of dark shadow. Although they are vulnerable to physical attack, these demons are able to drain the life from all that they touch, enveloping smaller demons until all they leave is a lifeless corpse. Cousin to the Sylph, these rare demons tend to live in the caves, swamps and other dark places of the ether.

Classification: *Elemental*

BASE MANA LEVEL: 62

MANA ABILITIES: Shadow Cloak, Life Drain

NATURAL SKILLS: Flying

RARITY: Rare

DIET: Carnivore

ATTACK/DEFENSE: 1. Shadow Cloak, 2. Envelop, 3. Life Drain

This rare elemental-class demon can be made from many different types of minerals, including clay, mud and sand, the most powerful of which is the stone. Juvenile Golems begin at only a few feet tall but can grow to over ten feet. They appear roughly humanoid, though they only have one large digit and an opposable thumb.

Classification: *Elemental*

BASE MANA LEVEL: 60	RARITY: Endangered
MANA ABILITIES: None	DIET: Herbivore
NATURAL SKILLS: Strength, Tough Skin	ATTACK/DEFENSE: 1. Fists, 2. Kick, 3. Tough Skin

HIPPOGRIFF—LEVEL 8

The Hippogriff is a hybrid of eagle and horse. Though fast on the ground, it lacks the fierce claws of its more powerful and rarer cousin, the Griffin, relying on strikes from its beak and hooves. It is a popular choice of demon for members of the Celestial Corps, second only to the Peryton.

Classification: *Aves*, *Equine*

BASE MANA LEVEL: 57

MANA ABILITIES: None

NATURAL SKILLS: Agility, Eyesight, Flying

RARITY: Migratory

DIET: Carnivore

ATTACK/DEFENSE: 1. Beak, 2. Kick

A Hydra is a large demon with three snakelike heads on long, flexible necks. Its body is similar to that of a monitor lizard, at around the same size of a large Canid. These demons were once more common in Hominum's part of the ether, but are now extremely rare.

Classification: *Reptilia*

BASE MANA LEVEL: 55	RARITY: Endangered
MANA ABILITIES: None	DIET: Carnivore
NATURAL SKILLS: Three Minds	ATTACK/DEFENSE: 1. Bite, 2. Claws

Another distant cousin to the Canid, the Lycan appears much like an Anubid, with a thicker, bulkier body and the head of a wolf. Though stronger than their cousins, they are less intelligent and difficult to control.

Classification: *Canidae*

BASE MANA LEVEL: 49	RARITY: Very Rare
MANA ABILITIES: None	DIET: Carnivore
NATURAL SKILLS: Acute Smell, Acute Hearing	ATTACK/DEFENSE: 1. Bite, 2. Claws

The Sylph is an elemental demon that is cousin to the Enenra, appearing as a faintly glowing specter that inhabits the clouds of the ether. Insubstantial as the mists they live in, these demons have no physical attack whatsoever. Instead, they are capable of healing themselves and others around them. Though delicate and easily injured by any object that passes through them, their high mana levels and rare healing ability makes them extremely desirable.

Classification: *Elemental*

BASE MANA LEVEL: 62	RARITY: Very Rare
MANA ABILITIES: Healing	DIET: Herbivore
NATURAL SKILLS: Flying	ATTACK/DEFENSE: 1. Healing, 2. Envelop

The Tarasque is a six-legged demon with a spiked tortoise shell, a club-tipped tail and a lizard-like head capped with a ridge of thick bone. They are able to survive in the hottest, most inhospitable of conditions, and their natural habitat is the Wurm-infested deserts of the ether. It is theorized that their spiked shells are designed to prevent Wurms from comfortably swallowing them.

Classification: *Reptilia*

BASE MANA LEVEL: 56	RARITY: Uncommon
MANA ABILITIES: None	DIET: Omnivore
NATURAL SKILLS: Armored Shell, Spikes	ATTACK/DEFENSE: 1. Armored Shell, 2. Bite, 3. Spikes

Once popular among orc shamans, Tikbalangs seem to have fallen out of fashion in recent years. Cousin to the Minotaur, these horse-headed demons share their larger cousins' aggression and prehensile hands. However, their body shape is more similar to that of a Wendigo, with long skinny arms that knuckle the ground.

Classification: *Equine*

BASE MANA LEVEL: 55	RARITY: Rare
MANA ABILITIES: None	DIET: Carnivore
NATURAL SKILLS: Agility, Strength, Prehensile Hands	ATTACK/DEFENSE: 1. Claws, 2. Fists

This rare, giant, furry creature inhabits the swamps of the ether. It is able to hold its breath for long periods of time, and its fur becomes so matted with moss and slime from its surroundings that it becomes camouflaged. Its preferred method of killing is drowning for smaller creatures, but it is also capable of using its two fangs to finish off tougher prey.

Classification: *Megafauns, Rodentia*

BASE MANA LEVEL: 64

MANA ABILITIES: None

NATURAL SKILLS: Camouflage,
Breath Holding

RARITY: Rare

DIET: Carnivore

ATTACK/DEFENSE:
1. Bite, 2. Claws

This humanoid shark demon is a favorite among orc shamans thanks to its vicious jaws, sharp claws and impressive agility. With a posture more akin to a chimpanzee than a man, these demons are excellent climbers and are capable of jumping great distances. They come in the various breeds of their animal counterparts, with the great white, hammerhead and tiger shark being the most common.

Classification: *Aquarine*

BASE MANA LEVEL: 61

MANA ABILITIES: None

NATURAL SKILLS: Agility, Climbing

RARITY: Rare

DIET: Carnivore

ATTACK/DEFENSE: 1. Bite, 2. Claws, 3. Tail Swipe

The most favored demon of the Celestial Corps, Perytons appear as winged, horse-sized stags, with majestic antlers branching from their foreheads. Their front legs end in hooves, yet their back legs are clawed like a falcon's, complete with deadly talons that can do serious damage. Instead of the traditional bob that all deers have, these demons have long, elegant tail feathers. While their herds migrate sporadically across Hominum's part of the ether, they are considered the most common of the flying steeds available to Hominum's summoners.

Classification: *Aves, Caprids*

BASE MANA LEVEL: 62

MANA ABILITIES: None

NATURAL SKILLS: Agility, Flying

RARITY: Migratory

DIET: Herbivore

ATTACK/DEFENSE: 1. Antlers, 2. Kick, 3. Talons

Sobeks are native to swamps, rivers and lakes, avoiding the wider seas and oceans of the ether. These thick-skinned bipedal crocodilians use their claws and jaws to tear apart their opponents, if their large tails haven't battered them to the ground first. Hunched over at five feet tall, this demon could stand toe-to-toe with its natural adversary, the Nanaue.

Classification: *Reptilia*

BASE MANA LEVEL: 62	RARITY: Common
MANA ABILITIES: None	DIET: Carnivore
NATURAL SKILLS: Swimming, Camouflage	ATTACK/DEFENSE: 1. Bite, 2. Claws, 3. Tail Swipe, 4. Thick Skin

Appearing as a giant bat with the musculature of a mountain gorilla, the Ahool is a solitary demon that is rarely found in the known ether. Ahools are occasionally used as a mount for more powerful orc shamans. Known for their acute senses of hearing and smell, they make excellent trackers on air and land alike. With sharp claws on its winged forelimbs and fangs as thick as elephant tusks, an Ahool is capable of taking on a Griffin.

Classification: *Rodentia*

BASE MANA LEVEL: 65

MANA ABILITIES: None

NATURAL SKILLS: Flying, Sonar, Night Vision, Hearing, Smell

RARITY: Very Rare

DIET: Omnivore

ATTACK/DEFENSE: 1. Fangs, 2. Claws

This rare demon will occasionally stray into Hominum's part of the ether. Horse-sized, it has the body, tail and back legs of a lion and the head, wings and talons of an eagle.

Classification: *Aves, Felidae*

BASE MANA LEVEL: 65

MANA ABILITIES: None

NATURAL SKILLS: Flying

RARITY: Migratory

DIET: Omnivore

ATTACK/DEFENSE: 1. Beak, 2. Claws, 3. Talons

Onis appear similar in size and stature to orcs and are a favored demon among veteran shamans. They are characterized by their crimson red skin, a pair of horns erupting from their foreheads and overdeveloped upper and lower canines. Though they appear bright, Onis are more animal than sentient being, with less intelligence than the average Mite.

Classification: *Apeish*

BASE MANA LEVEL: 70	RARITY: Rare
MANA ABILITIES: None	DIET: Omnivore
NATURAL SKILLS: Strength	ATTACK/DEFENSE: 1. Bite, 2. Horn, 3. Punch

This swamp-dwelling demon appears as a four-legged eel. Their lightning ability is coveted, but since they can only briefly leave the water before drying out, they are impractical for most summoners. Other than electric shock attacks, their preferred weapons are their serrated teeth, which are so dirty that they cause immediate infection. An Abaia can track bitten prey for days, waiting for them to sicken and die.

Classification: *Aquarine*

BASE MANA LEVEL: 80

MANA ABILITIES: Lightning

NATURAL SKILLS: Swimming, Amphibious, Immune to Lightning

RARITY: Uncommon

DIET: Carnivore

ATTACK/DEFENSE: 1. Infectious Bite, 2. Lightning

A close cousin to the Manticore and Criosphinx, the Chimera is a hybrid of lion, goat and snake. Its head is grotesquely deformed; the lower jaws and face appearing leonine but with a goat's eyes, horns and upper snout fused above as if it were a conjoined twin. The hybridization continues on the rest of the body, with its back legs hooved and its front paws clawed like a feline's. The tail appears as a prehensile green-scaled snake, complete with a venomous head.

Classification: *Caprids, Felidae, Reptilia*

BASE MANA LEVEL: 77

MANA ABILITIES: None

NATURAL SKILLS: Climbing, Prehensile Tail

RARITY: Very Rare

DIET: Omnivore

ATTACK/DEFENSE: 1. Bite, 2. Claws, 3. Venomous Fangs

These humanoid demons are tall, large, hairy and muscular. They have the head of a bull and cloven hooves for feet. Unlike the Golem, they have clawed hands, which are capable of manipulating weapons, though teaching one to use them is a difficult task. It is very rare to see one of these in Hominum's part of the ether.

Classification: *Caprids*

BASE MANA LEVEL: 72

MANA ABILITIES: None

NATURAL SKILLS: Strength

RARITY: Very Rare

DIET: Omnivore

ATTACK/DEFENSE: 1. Horns, 2. Claws, 3. Fists

The Nandi might be described as a giant, bearlike creature, with powerful jaws and claws that can tear apart most opponents. However, it has a musculature, intelligence and agility more akin to a dog's than that of a bear.

Classification: *Megafauns*

BASE MANA LEVEL: 75	RARITY: Very Rare
MANA ABILITIES: None	DIET: Omnivore
NATURAL SKILLS: Strength	ATTACK/DEFENSE: 1. Bite, 2. Claws

This rare demon has batlike wings and forelimbs, a scorpion tail and the body of a lion, though the dark fur is interspersed with sharp spines. The Manticore's leonine face can sometimes appear almost human, and its features are capable of expressing complex emotion. Its venom is so potent that one droplet will kill a man within minutes. Members of the Raleigh family are said to be immune.

Classification: *Arthropidae, Felidae*

BASE MANA LEVEL: 85

MANA ABILITIES: None

NATURAL SKILLS: Flying

RARITY: Very Rare

DIET: Carnivore

ATTACK/DEFENSE: 1. Bite, 2. Claws, 3. Spines, 4. Venomous Sting

The Ifrit is an elemental akin to the Golem, aligned with fire rather than stone. A close cousin to the ice-powered Jotun, its skin appears to be made of blazing lava. This fire elemental is immensely strong and is even capable of breathing flames from its mouth. It is one of the more powerful demons that orc shamans are able to capture from their part of the ether.

Classification: *Elemental*

BASE MANA LEVEL: 91	RARITY: Endangered
MANA ABILITIES: Flame	DIET: Omnivore
NATURAL SKILLS: Strength,	ATTACK/DEFENSE: 1. Flame,
Immune to Fire	2. Fists

JOTUN—LEVEL 13

Jotuns are known only from a fleeting mention in a single ancient Elven scroll, though Hominum's scholars dispute the authenticity of this text. Described as giant humanoids that appear to be hewn from ice, they are said to be capable of freezing all that they touch. These demons are suspected of living in the snowy ice caps of the ether's tallest mountains.

Classification: *Elemental*

BASE MANA LEVEL: 91

MANA ABILITIES: Frost

NATURAL SKILLS: Strength, Immune to Frost

RARITY: Endangered

DIET: Omnivore

ATTACK/DEFENSE: 1. Fists, 2. Frost

The Shen is similar to a giant clam, complete with a spherical, hinged shell. It moves on both land and sea by rolling itself back and forth. This demon has an enormous amount of mana, required for its unusual mirage spell—an ability that allows the Shen to create an illusion, usually of another, more powerful demon. It is not clear whether the Shen is actually creating an image or making those that are watching hallucinate, but the effect remains the same. Unfortunately, this demon is perhaps one of the rarest around, with only one recorded capture in all of Hominum's history. It died shortly after being checked against a fulfilmeter, but its shell remains at Vocans Academy to this day.

Classification: *Aquarine*

BASE MANA LEVEL: Unknown

MANA ABILITIES: Illusion

NATURAL SKILLS: None

RARITY: Endangered

DIET: Omnivore

ATTACK/DEFENSE: 1. Illusion,
2. Shell Snap

The Wendigo is a rare demon that is known to follow the Shrike migration across the ether, eating the carcasses of its victims. Despite its role as a carrion eater, the Wendigo is a powerful beast in its own right, with corded muscle lining its skinny frame. Standing as high as eight feet tall, it has branching antlers, a wolflike head and long arms that it uses to knuckle the ground like a gorilla. It is known to have the mottled gray skin of a corpse and the stench to match, most likely from its regular consumption of rotting flesh.

Classification: *Canidae, Caprids*

BASE MANA LEVEL: 90

MANA ABILITIES: None

NATURAL SKILLS: Agility, Strength

RARITY: Very Rare

DIET: Carnivore

ATTACK/DEFENSE: 1. Antlers, 2. Bite, 3. Claws

These enormous demons have the long necks and large bodies of giraffes, but with thicker limbs, a long tapering tail and a head that is more akin to that of a horse's or camel's. Their fur is short, gray and mottled with black patches. Traveling in herds of twenty or more, Indriks migrate widely, acting as a food source for the large, carnivorous demons across the ether's ecosystem. Given their role as prey animals and their high summoning level, these demons are relatively useless to summoners.

Classification: *Equine*

BASE MANA LEVEL: 75	RARITY: Common
MANA ABILITIES: None	DIET: Herbivore
NATURAL SKILLS: None	ATTACK/DEFENSE: 1. Stomp

AKHLUT—LEVEL 15

The Nanaue is to a shark as the Akhlut is to an orca, or killer whale. Cousin to the dolphin-like Encantado, this demon is thought to move on all fours like a wolf, using its webbed claws and fluked tail to travel over land and sea. As large as their animal counterparts, these demons have never been seen in the flesh. All knowledge of the Akhluts' existence comes from a depiction—a name and summoning level painted on the inside of an orc shaman's hut.

Classification: *Aquarine*

BASE MANA LEVEL: 100	RARITY: Rare
MANA ABILITIES: None	DIET: Carnivore
NATURAL SKILLS: Swimming	ATTACK/DEFENSE: 1. Bite 2. Claws, 3. Tail Swipe

WYVERN—LEVEL 15

The Wyvern is the orcs' main counter to the demons of the
Celestial Corps. These enormous scaled creatures have batlike
wings, long, spiked tails and horned crocodilian heads. Their
skin is so tough and cartilaginous that only a lance or
well-placed musket ball can pierce it. Other than their
jaws, the Wyverns' main weapons are their powerful
legs, which are tipped with the hooked hind claws
of a raptor. They are slower than most flying
demons and are often backed up by the
more agile Shrikes, Strixes and Vesps.

Classification: *Reptilia*

BASE MANA LEVEL: 105

MANA ABILITIES: None

NATURAL SKILLS: Flying,
Armored Skin

RARITY: Very Rare

DIET: Carnivore

ATTACK/DEFENSE: 1. Bite, 2. Horns,
3. Talons, 4. Armored Skin,
5. Tail Swipe

This amphibious demon could be described as a hybrid between a tortoise and a turtle, with webbed claws, a sharp beak and a protective shell. Their newborns appear the same size as a sea turtle, but they can grow to the dimensions of a small archipelago. In fact, they are often mistaken for islands, given the amount of vegetation that forms on their rugged shells. Considered the most long-lived demons in the ether, these demons are said to reach as old as two millennia.

Classification: *Reptilia*

BASE MANA LEVEL: 120

MANA ABILITIES: None

NATURAL SKILLS: Swimming

RARITY: Rare

DIET: Herbivore

ATTACK/DEFENSE: 1. Beak, 2. Shell

The Phantaur is as much an elephant as a Minotaur is a bull. With its serrated tusks, sturdy fists and a height of over ten feet, it is a force to be reckoned with. Thought to be the rarest and most powerful demon available to orc shamans, only one has ever been seen. Little is known of its behavior and habitat. It is thought that the one Phantaur to have been captured has been passed down through thousands of generations of shamans, its origins lost to the mists of time.

Classification: *Megafauns*

BASE MANA LEVEL: Unknown	RARITY: Endangered
MANA ABILITIES: None	DIET: Herbivore
NATURAL SKILLS: Long Reach, Strength	ATTACK/DEFENSE: 1. Thick Skin, 2. Trunk, 3. Tusk, 4. Punch

This demon roamed the ether thousands of years ago but is now extinct. Little is known about them, since all that remains are their bones. At twenty times the size of an elephant, these demons were gigantic, second only in size to the Zaratans, though from examination of their teeth it is theorized that they were peaceful herbivorous ruminants, grazing on treetops as a cow might eat grass. The Behemoth had a similar body structure to a hippo and a head comparable to that of a manatee.

Classification: *Megafauns*

BASE MANA LEVEL: Unknown	RARITY: Extinct
MANA ABILITIES: Unknown	DIET: Herbivore
NATURAL SKILLS: Unknown	ATTACK/DEFENSE: 1. Stomp

Previously unknown to Hominum's summoners, the Drake is something of a mystery to researchers at Vocans, since it is yet to be examined or tested against a fulfilmeter. From the descriptions of the owner of the only known specimen—one Fletcher Raleigh—it is clearly the first stage in the metamorphosis of a Salamander, facilitated by the extreme heat of a volcano. Somewhat larger than a Griffin, the Drake is similarly proportioned to that of a Salamander, with the addition of a long, sinuous neck, two back-facing horns on its head and a pair of large leathery wings. As with their smaller counterparts, Drakes have the ability to breathe fire, self-heal and heal others with their saliva. Rumors have circulated that a Drake's summoner becomes immune to fire, but the veracity of these claims is yet to be determined.

Classification: *Reptilia*

BASE MANA LEVEL: Unknown

MANA ABILITIES: Fire Breathing, Healing

NATURAL SKILLS: Flying, Agility, Fireproof

RARITY: Extremely Rare

DIET: Carnivore

ATTACK/DEFENSE: 1. Fire Breath, 2. Tail Spike, 3. Claws, 4. Beak

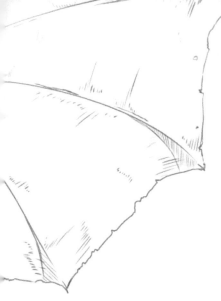

DRAGON—LEVEL UNKNOWN

According to the testimony of one Fletcher Raleigh, the Dragon is the final stage in the metamorphosis of the Salamander species. Appearing as a giant Drake, this demon is complemented by larger horns and scaly skin that is extremely difficult to penetrate. Only one specimen is thought to have existed—belonging to Khan, the religious leader of the orcs. It is theorized that only an albino orc is capable of summoning a demon of such power, stemming from the hypothesis that a quirk of evolution has given the albinos of the orc species immensely high fulfilment levels.

Classification: *Reptilia*

BASE MANA LEVEL: Unknown

MANA ABILITIES:
Fire Breathing, Healing

NATURAL SKILLS: Flying, Agility, Fireproof

RARITY: Extremely Rare

DIET: Carnivore

ATTACK/DEFENSE: 1. Fire Breath, 2. Tail Spike, 3. Claws, 4. Beak, 5. Armor Plating

Few sightings of this demon have been made, but most reports describe the Trunko as a white, whalelike creature with a trunk like an elephant's. Trunkos use these trunks to discreetly replenish their air reserves when they are at the surface, rather than breaching and allowing predator demons to know their presence. It is suspected that the Trunko is hunted by most sea predators, for their half-eaten remains have been known to wash up on the shore.

Classification: *Aquarine*

BASE MANA LEVEL: Unknown

MANA ABILITIES: Unknown

NATURAL SKILLS: Swimming

RARITY: Very Rare

DIET: Unknown

ATTACK/DEFENSE: Unknown

Not much is known about the Wurm, though a few notes can be found in the journals of Hominum's summoners, based on the infusion memories of their demons. The Wurm is native to the more arid parts of the ether, traveling alone beneath the ground. When it senses tremors above it, the blind demon bursts out from below and swallows its prey whole. Based on the rough sketches available, the demon has a long segmented exoskeleton and a round mouth full of serrated teeth. They can grow so large as to fill the moat around Vocans, tail to tip.

Classification: *Reptilia*

BASE MANA LEVEL: Unknown

MANA ABILITIES: Unknown

NATURAL SKILLS: Burrowing, Sense Tremors

RARITY: Very Rare

DIET: Carnivore

ATTACK/DEFENSE: 1. Bite, 2. Swallow

THE ESSENTIAL LIST OF SPELLS

Though there are thousands of spells available to summoners, few are useful in a battle situation. Below are a set of the most important spells for a battlemage to be aware of, compiled by James Baker and updated by Electra Mabosi, alchemist at Vocans Academy. It is important to note that several of these spells were discovered by James Baker in his study of orcish culture.

—Dame Fairhaven

Wyrdlight

The wyrdlight is the first spell a summoner learns, producing raw mana from their fingertip. Wyrdlight can be shaped into a ball and controlled with the summoner's mind, or left to float aimlessly around the room. These balls will dissipate when they touch another spell or another object. Alternatively, wyrdlight can be blasted out of one's finger to blind an enemy, though this is a wasteful use of mana considering the alternatives.

MANA COST—*very low*

SYMBOL COMPLEXITY—*0/10*

DIFFICULTY TO MASTER—*1/10*

Fire

One of the four battle spells most commonly used among summoners, the fire spell is useful in that the attacks can be easily shaped into beams, waves or blasts of flame, though a summoner can only direct the spell in an approximately straight line.

MANA COST—*medium*

SYMBOL COMPLEXITY—*6/10*

DIFFICULTY TO MASTER—*4/10*

Telekinesis

Perhaps the most useful of the battle spells, it is often used in emergencies to blast aside opponents in a wasteful but effective attack. Summoners who are particularly adept with this spell are able to move objects around them, creating a lasso of sorts to move them.

MANA COST—*medium*

SYMBOL COMPLEXITY—*3/10*

DIFFICULTY TO MASTER—*5/10*

Lightning

Most commonly used to tackle multiple opponents, the lightning spell is capable of jumping between foes. However, the spell kills only when expending a great deal of mana—otherwise, it will only stun the enemy.

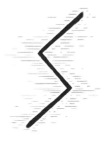

MANA COST—*high*

SYMBOL COMPLEXITY—*3/10*

DIFFICULTY TO MASTER—*5/10*

Shield

The shield is one of the most versatile of a battlemage's spells. It is particularly hard to master, since it must be shaped carefully with the summoner's mind. A shield spell can protect its summoner from enemy spells, projectiles and even blows from a sword of mace, but its durability is determined by its thickness, so a balance must often be struck between surface area and depth. Shields will crack or even shatter under too much trauma, and demons are capable of shredding through them with the slightest touch—the demonic energy that forms their bodies is lethal to them. One additional benefit of a shield is that it is able to be reabsorbed into the body, allowing the summoner to return most of the mana they used in creating it.

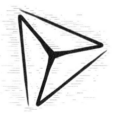

MANA COST—*medium*

SYMBOL COMPLEXITY—*7/10*

DIFFICULTY TO MASTER—*7/10*

Healing

The healing spell is a blessing to summoners, though it does have some drawbacks. Its mana cost is extremely high, it can leave scarring if applied too late after the wound, and it is dangerous to use near broken bones—the spell will sometimes cause the bones to fuse or regrow in dangerous ways, leaving the summoner permanently crippled or maimed, or in extreme cases, it can even cause death.

MANA COST—*very high*

SYMBOL COMPLEXITY—*5/10*

DIFFICULTY TO MASTER—*5/10*

Barrier

The barrier spell protects the skin from being cut, like a very flexible shield that sheathes around a body. Just as a shield spell does, it protects from attack spells and is ineffective against the touch of a demon. It is most useful as a deterrent from projectiles or close combat weapons. These will still do blunt-force damage, but a sword blow that might cut off an arm will instead break it, as if a bar of metal has struck. The spell is so complex that it requires at least four summoners to create an effective barrier. Across history, Hominum's kings have used the spell to protect themselves from assassination to this day, keeping a bodyguard of several summoners nearby to maintain its effect.

MANA COST—*high*

SYMBOL COMPLEXITY—*9/10*

DIFFICULTY TO MASTER—*9/10*

Amplify

The amplify spell is most often used by officers to increase the volume of their voices so that they can give orders to their men in the heat of battle, though they must balance this against the danger of alerting the enemy to their movements. Recently, the spell has been used to allow scrying crystals to replicate sounds that their bonded demons hear through vibration.

MANA COST—*very low*

SYMBOL COMPLEXITY—*2/10*

DIFFICULTY TO MASTER—*3/10*

Muffle

The antithesis to the amplify spell, the muffle spell can make the surrounding area quieter, if not completely silent. Though it's most useful when being used to avoid detection on a night raid, it is not unheard of for teachers at Vocans to use the spell when the students are particularly unruly.

MANA COST—*very low*

SYMBOL COMPLEXITY—*2/10*

DIFFICULTY TO MASTER—*3/10*

Growth

Upon its discovery by Electra Mabosi, Vocans's alchemist, the growth spell was heralded as the solution for hunger all across Hominum. However, it was soon discovered that the mana cost of such a spell was far too high for such applications. Its main practical application appears to be growing the *Medusa* plant, as

 demonstrated by Fletcher Raleigh, Cress Freyja, Sylva Arkenia and Othello Thorsager in their record-breaking time spent in the ether.

MANA COST—*very high*

SYMBOL COMPLEXITY—*7/10*

DIFFICULTY TO MASTER—*3/10*

Illusion

The illusion spell symbol is unknown. Vocans is only aware of its existence due to historic encounters in the ether with the rare Shen demon, a creature that can create strange visions for prey and predator alike. It is not clear whether the spell creates an actual image in the air or is simply a hallucination caused by the spell itself. For now, it has been classified as an illusion and shall remain that way until a specimen can be captured and dissected.

MANA COST—*unknown*

SYMBOL COMPLEXITY—*unknown*

DIFFICULTY TO MASTER—*unknown*

Strengthen

The strengthen spell is sometimes confused with the beserk spell, but is in fact only effective against nonorganic matter. Historically it was most often used on weapons and armor before a battle, duel or tournament to prevent them from chipping or shattering, but this practice has fallen out of favor given the high mana cost of the spell and its short lifespan, lasting only for approximately an hour and swiftly becoming less effective throughout. The barrier spell has replaced the strengthen spell's use on armor in tournaments. In organized duels it is only used when a companion is there to use their mana instead. During battle it is considered a waste, with other spells being more cost effective.

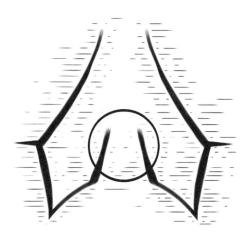

MANA COST—*high*

SYMBOL COMPLEXITY—*5/10*

DIFFICULTY TO MASTER—*5/10*

Mist

This spell is almost never used due to its complexity, the high mana cost and its relatively useless applications. It is able to draw moisture from the surrounding air to create a mist. The size, shape and longevity of this mist is determined by the skill of the summoner and the humidity of the environment. Some summoners have used this spell to create clean drinking water in a survival situation, concentrating the mist into a ball of liquid above a container. This is an emergency measure, as it would likely take up all the summoner's mana to do so.

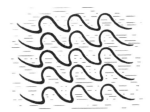

MANA COST—*very high*

SYMBOL COMPLEXITY—*8/10*

DIFFICULTY TO MASTER—*8/10*

Frost

The frost spell is a recent discovery and has yet to be tested more than a few times on the field of battle. It is most effective in humid or wet environments, turning the moisture into ice, though even in dry conditions it can freeze and shatter an orc's limb with enough mana.

MANA COST—*medium*

SYMBOL COMPLEXITY—*8/10*

DIFFICULTY TO MASTER—*7/10*

Ethereal Blade

The ethereal blade is an emergency measure, using a solid white substance to form a double-edged sword of sorts, fixed around the hand used to perform the spell. Though its edges and point are sharp enough to cut, it is easily shattered and is a poor substitute for any other blade. It is also near-useless against demons, dissipating into white light upon contact.

MANA COST—*high*

SYMBOL COMPLEXITY—*4/10*

DIFFICULTY TO MASTER—*6/10*

Darkness Cloak

This spell was discovered when a summoner named James Baker dissected an Enenra. It has an extremely high mana cost and is complex to etch, but it is occasionally used in battle when the situation warrants it. Darkness cloak literally shadows an area in darkness, hiding those within from sight. It is only effective at night, for during the day the spell will not completely obscure everything within it and the strange shadow effect draws too much attention.

Berserk

The berserk spell is extremely dangerous and should only be used in the most dire of circumstances. The spell caster will gain boundless energy and significantly greater strength, its duration and potency determined by the amount of mana used. However, this comes at a cost. Once the spell has run its course, the summoner will become exhausted. It is not unheard of for a battlemage to fall unconscious in the midst of battle and remain so for several days after the use of this spell, if not collapsing to the ground and being unable to move for several hours. In some cases, where too much mana was used, the user will die. The mana needed for the spell to be effective is surprisingly low, but the amount used is hard to regulate, making it a risky spell to use. It is recommended that summoners always train in this spell with a companion to watch over them and even then to only do so when their mana levels are low, so as not to accidentally use too much and do themselves injury.

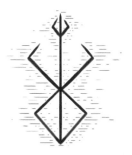

MANA COST—*low*

SYMBOL COMPLEXITY—*7/10*

DIFFICULTY TO MASTER—*8/10*

Anesthesia

This spell is rarely taught at Vocans, given that the healing spell will usually fix most injuries, making the anesthesia spell moot. It has a high mana cost, making it a poor solution for those with long-term chronic pain. However, should there be an injury that a healing spell cannot fix, such as a broken bone, disease or poisoning, and the summoner has no need of their mana at that time, it is possible to provide temporary pain relief through the use of this spell.

MANA COST—*high*

SYMBOL COMPLEXITY—*6/10*

DIFFICULTY TO MASTER—*7/10*

Detect Life

This spell is most often used by veteran summoners when hunting for new demons in the jungles of the ether, but it is rarely taught at Vocans anymore due to its difficulty to master, even when studied over several years. Once cast on a living creature, including the summoner themselves, that individual will be able to see nearby living creatures as surrounded by a yellow glow, making it easier for them to track prey. The effect is temporary, usually lasting no more than thirty seconds, but can be useful to use periodically on night watch to help track enemy movements when the cat's-eye spell will not suffice.

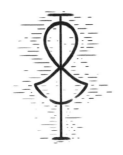

MANA COST—*high*

SYMBOL COMPLEXITY—*8/10*

DIFFICULTY TO MASTER—*9/10*

Tighten Knot

This spell is extremely simple and is mostly used by lazy summoners when tying their laces, though it has been found to be helpful on ships during strong winds. It is also useful when used in conjunction with the ethereal threads spell.

MANA COST—*low*

SYMBOL COMPLEXITY—*2/10*

DIFFICULTY TO MASTER—*2/10*

Loosen Knot

This is the antithesis of the tighten spell. Though simple, it has saved a few summoners' lives, especially when being held captive by orcs, though it is hard to perform when their hands are bound. Unfortunately, the focus on the four primary battle spells at Vocans has led to novice summoners forgetting this spell, even when it might help them escape.

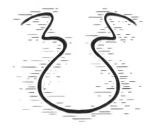

MANA COST—*low*

SYMBOL COMPLEXITY—*2/10*

DIFFICULTY TO MASTER—*2/10*

Unlock

It is not known where this spell came from, since it would have no natural applications in the ether. Nevertheless, it has been found in even the most ancient of spell books and allows a summoner to open any lock. This has led to summoners using bars to keep their doors secure, since the spell does not work on those.

MANA COST—*low*

SYMBOL COMPLEXITY—*2/10*

DIFFICULTY TO MASTER—*2/10*

Ethereal Threads

Found within a dissected Arach demon, a sticky, glowing gossamer-like substance can be ejected from a summoner's fingers and used to ensnare opponents. The substance will eventually dissolve, so it will only keep an enemy bound for so long, but it is a useful spell that some summoners have argued should be added to the list of the first spells a novice summoner learns.

MANA COST—*medium*

SYMBOL COMPLEXITY—*6/10*

DIFFICULTY TO MASTER—*7/10*

Cat's Eye

The cat's-eye spell looks almost exactly like its namesake, a thin oval within a circle. The spell produces yellow light that must be shone directly into its user's retinas. The summoner's eyes will turn feline in appearance, which can be very disconcerting, but it comes with the advantage of giving the summoner far better night vision.

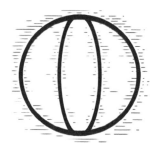

MANA COST—*low*

SYMBOL COMPLEXITY—*4/10*

DIFFICULTY TO MASTER—*4/10*

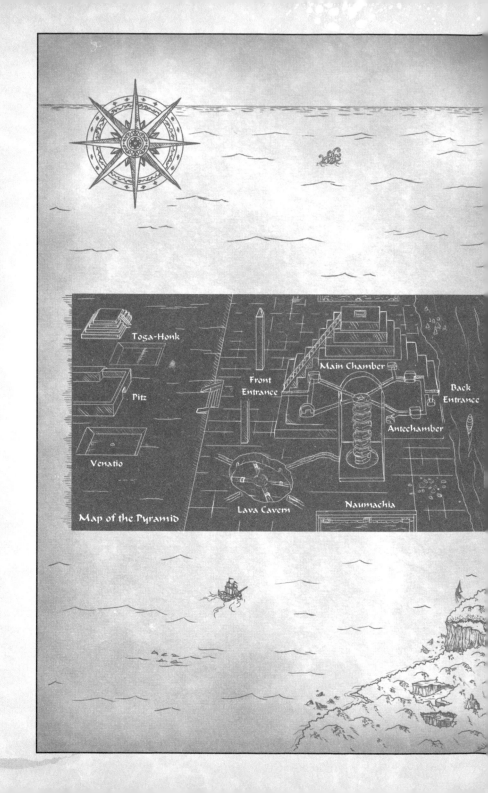

Map of Hominum

Elven Lands

Akhad Desert

Pelt

Beartooth Mountains

Boreas

Corcillum

Antioch

Vesanian Sea

Vocans Academy

Raleighshire

Orc Jungle

The Pyramid

The Warren

The Waterfall

The Swamps